MARY'S BOY, JEAN-JACQUES

MARY'S BOY, JEAN-JACQUES

and other stories

Vincent O'Sullivan

TE HERENGA WAKA
UNIVERSITY PRESS

Te Herenga Waka University Press
Victoria University of Wellington
PO Box 600, Wellington
New Zealand
teherengawakapress.co.nz

Te Herenga Waka University Press
was formerly Victoria University Press.

ISBN 9781776920006

A catalogue record is available from the
National Library of New Zealand

Acknowledgements
'Splinters' was first published in *Landfall* 239, edited by Emma Neale
(2020), and 'Ko tēnei, ko tēnā' in *Middle Distance: Long Stories
of Aotearoa New Zealand*, edited by Craig Gamble (2021).
Grateful thanks to the editors.

Printed in Singapore by Markono Print Media Ltd Pte

for Barry Cleavin and Denise Copland

Contents

GOOD FORM

Andrew thinks back to what it was like before his medication. There is a pleasure he takes from remembering he cannot explain. Nor is there need to. Two lives which are one. A sense of achievement, even to think that. Being able to say so.

He is looking at the blue drapes. The half inch of brilliant morning where the edges fail to meet. The light falls on a vase of flowers that flares with purples and reds. Alison would have done that on purpose, would have known where the light would fall by the time he woke.

Alison was five when he was born. There were few children their age on neighbouring farms, so they saw little of others apart from the hours at school, and on the bus that picked them up near the Norfolk pine, and let them off, on the other side of the road, late in the afternoon. Daddy did not think much of their neighbours in any case. There were Dutch immigrants on one side, and a ropey lot, as he called them, on the slope of the other side leading down to the river. Four miles away at the turn-off, D'Arcy's store sold everything from hoops of fencing wire to mint-flavoured toothpaste. Ed D'Arcy painted small scenery pictures that he put on the walls and once in a blue moon some stranger might purchase one. His wife's hair was light-coloured and piled high, but if you called after-hours or on Sundays you might see her with it let down to her waist. For Andrew and Alison, 'out for a treat' meant a drive down to D'Arcys for the homemade ice cream that people even came out from town to get during the summer.

11

Sometimes but not often letters arrived with interesting stamps. Daddy had two uncles in Inverness. They were very old and did not have families of their own. They wrote on the backs of cards things that never said very much, like 'Still ticking along', or 'Welcome anytime'. Daddy looked at them and put them on the mantel above the fireplace for a week or two, but it was their mother who wrote back thanking them. Careful to put 'UK' on the envelope, although Daddy, the rare times that he wrote, wrote 'Scotland'.

Once, Andrew said, after listening at school to those who went off to stay with cousins, or for holidays at beaches, 'There's not many of us are there? Our family, like?' His mother told him quietly that if God had wanted them to be more then there would be. Which wasn't much of an answer. Their father drew his thick eyebrows together, which always made the children laugh, and said, 'He sometimes gets some things right.' That was God, he meant. Their mother stood up and cleared the table, and so often it was like that, Daddy or their mother saying things that made the other answer in a way that stopped other things being said. As Alison so much later said to Andrew, 'Nobody fought and nobody didn't fight. That was worst of all.' And Andrew, always not wanting things to be as bad as they were, said, 'At least we had dogs and horses.'

By then Andrew was nine and Alison was fourteen. When he wasn't working on the farm Daddy spent a lot of time with Alison and her pony. He drove the green float to gymkhanas, and Alison's bedroom walls were hung with bunches of red and blue ribbons. Their mother bred sheep for a special kind of wool but was never very successful. She said she should go to a week-long course at Massey but Daddy told her you become an expert by doing things, not sitting in

12

a classroom writing stuff down.

The school told his parents that Andrew was a clever boy. He had a future. It was a phrase that puzzled him. Everyone had a future or they'd be dead already. It still amuses him. He thinks of it now, as he looks at his watch, which he placed under his pillow before he slept. The habits that last a lifetime. He hears Alison moving about in the kitchen, which is beneath his bedroom. He showers in a bathroom that has blue and white tiles she bought in a Turkish shop in Melbourne. He marvels at what she has made of the old house. Or the new house, one probably should say. It is far more than simply the old house done over.

Alison has made a lot of money. Mum's 'messing about with wool' really came to something, once Alison decided that was what she wanted to be good at. Look at her now. Exports. Fashion lines. Italian fabrics. Her own brand, which apparently means a lot. He's happy to be surprised whenever he walks through the rooms that are the same as when he was young, and yet so very different. The altered angles to some of the walls. Big windows that, as Alison says, let the weather inside. The primary colours where drab wallpapers had been. Almost too bright, you think at first, and yet no, you give them time to work on you, you see they are fine as they are. As is the long plain table in the kitchen, and the vivid blue crockery, and the two canaries in a large cage, singing their hearts out. He asked her what their names were, these birds? She told him, 'A and B.' It didn't matter if you confused them, near identical as they were. Andrew said, 'But the letters must stand for something?' She laughed and called him an old pedant. 'Then what a choice you have.'

———

Alison means more to Andrew than anyone he knows. His wife, whom he no longer lives with, but nor, as she insists, are they seriously apart, understood that from the start. 'It may sound odd but it is important that you know,' he had said to her. His wife, who is French, says, should conversation about her husband turn too serious, it was better not to stir the wasp's nest of the Anglo-Saxon mind. Or she would say, with what some think an affected Gallic shrug, 'Another country, another man.' Which could mean, or not mean, almost anything.

People who first meet Alison assume she is married, or at one time must have been. She is tall, with tightly curled fair hair, and features that Andrew, during his years in Europe, sometimes saw in early paintings of the Virgin—both calm and resolutely tough. When people learn that she is immovably single, most men think what a waste, and some of her women friends envy her. Not that she speaks to anyone of reasons for being so. That is the way it is, as if like her weight, or her height. Describing her, but not defining.

'My God,' Andrew says, as he comes into the north-facing kitchen. 'It really is so lovely.' Here, he means, where they stand. But there too, outside the large window—the planting she has done over the years on the tilt of the slope down towards the road, so changing the scraggy paddocks from when they were young. Andrew tells her, 'We are the only two who see both at once. Then and now.'

Alison disappoints him, just a little. 'One, thank goodness, overgrows the other.'

She is here eight months of the year, the other four travelling, the cosmopolitan as most of her friends see her. 'Back in the valley' is what she and Andrew refer to as her time here at home. Back in the district, the small town twelve

14

kilometres away, the place where stories are told about them to newcomers, *the* story from thirty years back. The guessing at why she does it, this rebuilding, this choosing to run a business that makes her a legend journalists want to probe at, her brilliance as a designer and not moving an inch from where she grew up. Bugger me, as the local men say, could have anything she wants and sticks to here, where everyone knows her. Likes her. Can't understand the first fucking thing about her. The women more inclined to guess at reasons. She's here because she is here. Leave it at that. But they never do. What folk don't know is too good not to wonder about. You spent five minutes chatting with either of them, the quiet brother on his rare trips back, his exuberant sister whose factory in the town has put the place on the map, not a flicker of airs and graces between them. First names like anyone else. But Jesus, hang on. You'd never call them 'like the rest of us'. Weird wasn't quite the word. Just too much of somewhere else about them. That was said right from way back. You'd be none the wiser whatever you were told.

The woundings of time. Alison and Andrew speak of it sometimes. He is here for only a few days each year. Sometimes it is longer than that between visits. There is no awkwardness if one of them starts speaking of it. Back then. Not that there is a deep urge to go over it. Going over changes nothing. The way their lives took such separate ways, the closeness that does not depend on their seeing each other. Together as now in one place. Together when they are not. Andrew at colleges in different places. He changes from one to another every few years. There are always places keen to have him. He is a big name too, in his way, although the valley is less aware of that. Just 'the clever brother', as he was called back then, when the farm was just that, the farm.

It was Andrew who first saw Hank Mexted driving past the milk stand to the end of the by-road, where he turned his quad bike and rode slowly back. All the time he was looking up to the old villa where they lived. Then the next afternoon the boy saw it over again, while his father was still across at the milking sheds. A few weeks later, when it was dark earlier, Andrew watched him yet again, the tall neighbour who now turned on a bright light mounted on the quad bike. He manoeuvred the long beam so it cut across the dusk and swept across the side of the house. Mum was in the kitchen, with Alison helping her, at the back of the house. There was an old roll blind above the window, but it was never let down. Andrew tried to tug at it once and it was too stiff to move. But Hank must have known only someone on the shed side of the house would see the light he was beaming up. Anyone in the kitchen would know nothing about it. So it must have been Dad he wanted to see it. Andrew understood nothing, apart from this being strange. He started to run towards the yards, but Dad took him by surprise, stepping from behind him. He felt the big hand fall on his shoulder. Before he knew what it was he wanted to ask, Dad said simply *Tsssk*, several times over, *tsssk*, the kind of noise he made when he was handling a skittish calf. When he did speak it was only to say, 'No need to mention this inside.' He was rubbing at his hands with a disinfected rag, the last thing he always did when he finished up in the sheds.

'Is that Mr Mexted?' the boy asked.

'Just get inside.'

He walked back to turn off the lights in the shed, brighter now that it was suddenly darker. As he got closer to the

16

hanging naked bulbs, his shadow pushed out longer towards where Andrew stood. For a moment it seemed very scary. He didn't like it either when Dad went like that, saying nothing. Alison had this saying at times like this: 'Thunder's on the way.' She laughed though when she said it. Nothing scared Alison.

Then it was Saturday, two weeks after the quad bike was first ridden up and down the road in front of the house. On the bus coming home from school the day before, Alison said to him, 'I think things might happen, Andrew, that we don't want to happen. We'll have to be brave about it.'

They sat where they always did at the back of the bus. The D'Arcy kids were brawling about a raincoat, still tugging at each other when the driver dropped them off at the store. How strange that things went on just a little way off that had nothing to do with us, and that feeling of loneliness as you watched it all taking place. Even watching those at home. Me here and everything else there. Andrew took Alison's fingers with his own and she squeezed them back. We are the Martins, as Daddy sometimes told them; we are different from other people round here. He did not say better but used words like 'depth' and 'background', and Andrew was none the wiser. His mother thought so too but for other reasons. Alison sometimes explained things to him, but not always. He knew early on that his mother was not at all like the mothers he saw picking up kids after school, talking with the teachers, to each other, making jokes with other children. He knew God had something to do with it, although thinking that was like when windows are fogged up. You rub a few inches of glass, you know a little about what is on the other side. Then thinking about things runs out. What you know just stops. But Alison was there for him. She squeezed his fingers back. She moved a fingernail against his palm until their game took over.

The Saturday when things fell apart. So much in one day. Dad said he had an old separator to drop off so he would toss it on the ute. He would take 'the outfit' with him, one of his words for the children when he was in a good mood. Or even 'the whole outfit', as though there were dozens of them. They would call in at D'Arcys for one of the passionfruit swills that people drove miles for. Then he would drive Andrew back so he could pile away the load of wood a workman had dropped in front of the shed earlier in the week. It was a boring job, but Dad said he would pay him two dollars for it. Andrew told Dad it was the biggest load they'd ever had dropped off, and his father said, 'One in that case if you're going to whinge.'

He would drop Alison off for her music lesson with a woman down the valley and wait to bring her home. He told them all this at breakfast. This is the plan, he said. Alison, who'd say anything, had even said to Dad once that he'd be Napoleon if it was only a matter of planning. Andrew had thought is she asking for it, but Daddy, as she always called him, was getting softer with her the older she got. Sometimes when nobody at home had said anything for days, she was the one to draw them together. Back to normal. She could do it with her mother as well, although it was further with Mum to bring her back.

You could tell this morning that Mum had been crying again. But nobody said much, there was no shouting or arguments, so it was hard to know what was wrong. Andrew knew she read very late at night because whenever he woke he saw the light on in the spare room opposite his own. She used to sleep in there some nights but now it seemed all the time. She read the Bible but there were other books too on the table by her bed, lives of people, she said; you could learn so much from other people, things about yourself you'd never otherwise think.

Alison was the one who seemed to understand things. Sometimes now on his visits back, as they sit so companionably together after dinner, their glasses like big rubies in the clever lighting, he will say what goodness knows he has told her often enough, 'You would all say things and I had no idea.'

His sister teases him. 'That's the trouble with smart people.' Not that they always go over things time and again. Pretty much everything about those old days has been said. This is so much later. They are happy to sit in silence, to listen to music together, to talk until the small hours if the mood takes them. To know they so love being together for short stints like this, as they know too how far distant their lives and interests are when they are not together.

Dad had dropped him back after the treat at D'Arcys. The boy stood at the great pile of pine, the rough pale blocks with the scent he loved breathing in. He takes up one by one the solid chunks and heaves them into the empty corrugated iron shed. At first the chunks of wood clang against the back wall as he tosses them in. He counts them as the pile grows. He slows down. He stops after a hundred to take a breather. His hands are hot inside the canvas gloves he wears against splinters. He hates the job. He is angry that Alison is off with Dad, having an easy time of it. After an hour the dumped wood is only halfway through. He takes off his gloves and tilts a bottle of cordial that is warm and tastes boring. He's always asking Mum but she never makes it stronger. Sugar is bad for us. Sweet things are bad for us. Your lovely teeth Andrew you don't want them ruined. Alison says he has to remember that is Mum's way of loving them. Some people are not great at saying so straight out so they say something else instead.

He rubs his hands against his jeans before picking up his gloves. He hears what must be a bird or an animal even tangled in something, but no, birds don't grieve like that. A high dense cry and then a drawn-out sound, a choked sound like something wanting to become words but unable to find them. He is struck with a feeling deeper than fright. As it comes again it is a cry that seems to drain colour from everything around him. He sees only a slowly billowed curtain lifting at the kitchen window. Everything else so still.

He has no awareness of his own rapid flowing into this new shaping of time. He is standing inside the kitchen doorway. His mother's head is turned towards him, her body rigid on its chair. She is looking towards him, her face that of a girl who has just been struck. They hold each other's gaze in this moment of such fragility, as if she is hoping to stall him as he is, to prevent whatever it is he shall next take in. The exact second as it were in which a mirror cracks. In later years, without his medication, that is the image, the moment, that surges back to him with such force he will physically crumple to a weeping child. Whatever his brilliance as the scholar he becomes, it will take weeks to retrieve him when such a crisis occurs.

The different things she needs for baking are spread on the kitchen table—the tin flour mill, the wooden rolling pin, a tin dish with scalloped shapes pressed into it. Ordinary things as witness. Saturday as it always was. But before he crosses the worn pattern of the kitchen lino, she raises the teatowel that some impulse of bizarre delicacy has made her place across her hand. The red mess beneath it spreading across the table. Andrew sees the upright handle of the knife

20

she has driven down through her hand, the blade clamping it to the table. He is now standing beside her. He draws her towards him, grasping at the yellow knife handle in one rapid move. The heat of her cheek through his shirt, the sag of her body against his. He tugs at the knife and draws it free. The drag of the little bones of her hand as the blade scrapes through them. Blood wells rapidly and pours from her hand. Blood from her wound runs along the wooden table to the spread square of flour. They come together forming runnels and small rolled clots.

He is not to be ashamed, his wife later so insists; there is no shame in therapy, any more than there is blame for so long ago. But he will tire of the professional phrases offered him, their banality, as he does of the sound of the words that are wrung out of him. He says, 'I am like wires that don't connect,' and his therapist tells him such picturings are simply displacements, metaphor another bandage to be dealt with. He makes fun of the doctor's own falling back on them. He changes from one clinic to another. That image of the wires persists with him. To be reconnected. To hear their reviving hum. You have to have some way to think of things, a shorthand for what is going wrong. He comes to accept that medication may not be a cure, but if it makes life tolerable, that is enough. Who has the right to expect more than enough?

After breakfast Andrew and Alison walk down to the old pond that is now the ornamental lake. His sister makes fun of what the contractor called it. 'It's still the old pond tarted up.' There was even an article about the old house and the way she has done it up, she tells him. In a posh Auckland magazine. 'Things you would never believe,' she says, 'extensive views,

21

imaginative planting, "the old and the new forming a unique statement both absorbing and interrogating both". It costs a lot of money to have experts write as badly as that.'

Andrew thinks back. 'Daddy never thought the place was good enough for us, of course.'

'Oh.' Alison smiles. 'Daddy fancied we had "form". Blood-wise. A notch up on the rabble. God knows where that came from.'

'We're safe now, mocking at a distance,' Andrew says. 'Notice the way we still call him Daddy whenever we talk about him?'

So much they assume as they walk on, side by side. It need not be spelled out yet again. Alison thinking how after the gunshot Daddy was more aloof than ever, more a cut above. Andrew not wanting it, yet the memory forcing itself on him. No wonder he makes his visits back so brief, even to the marvellously different world Alison has made of it. However close they are. Need each other. However much. Later in the day that never ends, that most of all re-emerging for him. Once Daddy and Alison came back. His mother talking but not making sense, not to the ambulance man and the woman with him, until the injection they gave her made her sleep. But just before she did, her pressing Andrew's hand so tightly his fingers hurt. Telling him again, telling the strangers as well, as if so urgent a thing they too should know, everyone should know. 'How much worse for him. How much worse. Not one but two. Both his hands for us.' Andrew's own hand drawn up against her cheek, before she slept.

They walk about the old farm that looks itself and yet is never the same. Mostly they walk in silence. Saying nothing means happy. The slope of the land, the shallow hill rising behind the house, the spread of farms stretching out on the flat. The stand of handsome trees not there twenty years ago, as if brought in from other places so more exotic than here was ever meant to be. The road in front of the house that has been sealed since back then. The Mexteds have left so long ago. Mrs Mexted dead. The D'Arcys too, although the shop is there still, pretty much the same, and still called D'Arcys. The ice cream Mrs D'Arcy perfected has been bought by a brand that markets it a hundred k's in every direction. There is so little Alison and Andrew might say that the other does not already know. It reminds him, yet again, of their sitting at the back of the school bus. So part of the world, of course, yet how easy to think it was not really theirs. They were always special. Always somewhere else.

They speak a little about their lives when they are not together. Andrew tells his sister about France, about the compromise of his marriage, his directing a research programme at Montpellier, the absurd amount of money they pay him to do so.

'Let alone the fame,' Alison says, pressing his arm.

'Oh yes.' Andrew smiles. 'We must never forget that.'

There is no need really to talk about his 'lapses', as he calls them, that seem to arrive every three or four years. He times his extended leave so his problems remain his own. He knows what steps to take. Nothing much will change. His psychiatrist, he jokes, is awfully proud of the chair he sits in during sessions. It was given to him by Freud's grandson. 'We all have our fetishes, even when they're not.'

Alison lights a Sobranie. Would you believe it, she is the only woman she likes who smokes? 'I could be into bestiality and no one would turn a hair. But *this*.' Her brother tells her he loves the smell of them. If he took up a vice that would be the first.

Before they return to the house she shows him 'the new shed', but it is so much more than that. An architect who won some award for it. Beautiful timber benches. Overhead lights that turn with the hour of the day for the winter months. Six local women work here, she says. She paid for them to attend expert courses in design, fabrics, even chemistry. There is nothing about wool they don't know, or what can be done with it. Sample bales are brought in from all over the country, and what is decided here goes on to the factory in town. 'They're obsessed as I am with what we do. The women here. They like it as much as I do that the local farmers thought I was certifiable when I started up. "Bringing wool into dairy country!"' The great bales brought up from the south. But cheaper by far than trying to do the same thing in the big smoke. 'We're good and we work fast. "From the Sheep to the Walkway in One Season". That's on our label.' And underneath, in smaller type, 'Merino Pure'.

The sky has clouded over when they leave the shed. The surface of the lake that was once a pond gives back a drab sky. The week after their mother was taken in the ambulance, and had not come back, Alison was standing exactly here when she heard the first shot from the road, sixty yards down from the house. The sound she understood without having to see the black quad bike, or the man who rode it. She ran and saw that he had passed the house and continued on towards where he would turn and drive back. His rifle was laid across his knees, as it had been those other times when he went past. But this was the first time he had raised it and fired towards the house.

Alison felt the pounding in her chest as she kept running to the back steps, not knowing that her father had turned the bathroom key to shut Andrew inside and then gone through

24

to the locker in the wash house that was always clasped with a padlock. No one could open it unless they knew the numbers to set on the little revolving wheels. Daddy took out the shotgun he had not handled since the end of the duck season.

By the time she reaches the house and leaps the three steps of the back porch, Daddy has left through the front door and covered half the distance towards the bright red splash of the tin letterbox. The quad bike has turned and is coming back, moving slowly enough that a man might almost keep up with it by walking. Daddy has stopped there, halfway down the drive, beside a large rusting drum. He holds his shotgun at an angle across his chest. Hank Mexted keeps on, so slowly Alison thinks he must be going to stop. But as he comes closer he raises his rifle and rests the butt on his knee. Daddy is doing nothing, just standing there, as if leaning on the drum, and now he raises the barrel but does not bother to look along it through the sights. He blasts more or less at random. There is a clang as the metal of the quad bike takes the impact. For a second the wheels veer crooked but Mr Mexted pulls the vehicle back. It comes in on Alison that what she is watching is a kind of game between her father and the man whose wife he visits, as her mother knew and Alison herself too, but only now the full adult enormity of it is clear to her. For Hank, their neighbour from two farms along, returns the shot with his own. Daddy drops his gun. He grasps with his freed hand at the drum's edge to prevent his falling. His other hand feeling at his leg, just above the knee. When Alison again looks to the road, the quad bike grows small as it keeps on in the other direction. It is all over. For the second time that week the ambulance races the eleven kilometres from town, its siren telling the world. She and Andrew do not go back to school for a week. An aunt comes to live with them. Daddy comes back in time, for the time he has.

It is here the story breaks into what became—for the district, for the farming families between here and town, for the town itself—a yarn to spin in the pub, a comic turn of one man hopping across the fences to get a slice of the other bloke's missus; and that other story entirely, of the right thing done, of honour, of where proper behaviour lies. For when Hank Mexted is almost level with the red slash of the letterbox, vivid as a rail signal in the diminishing dusk, he knows with the suddenness of an electric jolt that fucken Martin had no intention to harm him with his own firing, that the aim from up the drive was deliberately, contemptuously, askew. There is rage in his own quick raising of his rifle, a careful and he hoped equally contemptuous decision merely to *make it clear* . . . Not giving the satisfaction of the worst, which he withheld. And so within days a story to amuse the city papers, this absurdly warped story of saving face, once it came out in court. This mad fucker, as Daddy so often was called, standing there waiting to be shot, a single blank already fired from the shotgun he carried to make it *seem* he was for real. But *demanding* he was shot in return! Daddy walking through some elevating drama of his own, showing how a 'gentleman' behaved, the fanciful description he bestows on himself, faced with trash like Mexted. When Alison and Andrew talked it through, so long ago, she had put it so simply. 'Daddy didn't even need to say it. Good form.'

Before he leaves next morning, Alison leans forward to kiss his cheek above the lowered car window. They already have held each other in a long embrace. Andrew has not said when he hopes to visit again, nor does she tell him when next she might be in Europe. In his part of Europe. Arrangements are never made ahead. Perhaps her good friend Celeste will be with her. Perhaps not. That kind of certainty does not concern them.

He waves from the old letterbox, still there beside the new, much larger one with its striking iridescent sign. Still painted its bright red, as it was when they were children. When it was the first thing to catch their eye, all that way ahead, as the school bus took the sharp turn and that was their own valley waiting for them. Their own farm.

Alison waves back.

SPLINTERS

One of the good things about growing old. Her sister Deb had been throwing such phrases about for the past ten years, since before she turned sixty. A flighty, trivial person since she first declared a teenager must be rebellious, and now thought a woman of a certain age—another favoured phrase—would naturally offer wise and interesting remarks. Deb was rich and had problems with her weight, but was kindly, and in several book clubs, and at least voted differently from her husband. Which did not mean for a moment she was not hard to take, almost impossible to like.

Emily realised she was taking a leaf from her sister's book as she looked past the young boy with the pale inquiring face who sat opposite her, to the back yard's tangle of unmown lawn, the shrubs gone wild, the snaggled macrocarpa rising behind it all. 'One of the bad things about getting old,' she heard herself saying, 'is that what used to be quite a pretty garden can get away on you.' She smiled at the pointlessness of saying this to her grandson, who was here to play draughts, which he was obsessed with, while waiting for his mother to pick him up after her appointment. Appointments were frequent but important. They kept caviar on the table, as his father Barry said, meaning it to be a joke, although Donald had no idea why that was funny. He knew though that 'appointments' meant his mother drove people to look at houses, and turned on taps and switches for them so they would know the house worked, and often there was a 'special occasion' when she sold one.

'It's your move, Emily,' the boy reminded her. It was special, he knew that, when he called his grandmother by her real name. Another sort of game between them. It showed what good mates they were. His mother said he shouldn't so he was careful it was only like now, with just the two of them together. His arms, in their grey school jersey with a monogram a bit like the crocodile on the shirt his father wore when he played golf, leaned to either side of the checkered board.

Chit of a thing, Emily thought. Made her think of a bird. As he pressed against her when Meg came to collect him and he said goodbye and thank you for having me, Gran, he might as well have been a bundle of twigs. Which of course was nonsense. He was dead keen on soccer, and whatever else it was he played. He liked to tell her but she wasn't always sure of what he said. 'Nifty', though. He told her that was one of the words the coach used about him. And solid. His defence was solid.

'Yes,' he said, 'there are some things you can't help being good at.'

The boy watched the board without looking up at her. He reached out to put his fingers on one of the pieces, then took them away. 'I've decided to think about it more carefully.' Then he asked her, 'How do you mean, "get away on you"?', bringing them back to that.

'It means it just grows all the time and next thing it's a mess.'

'We've got a man comes in and cuts our lawns. The hedges and things. This big mower. And the clipper works by itself. He holds it and it just goes along the hedge.'

Emily made out her next move was harder to decide on than it was. 'Just get Dave to do it,' Donald said about the garden. 'I can ask him.'

'The trouble is,' his grandmother said, 'I've come to like it like that. The birds love it that way too. Things can be too tidy.'

'And cats, I bet,' Donald said. 'They'd love it like that. Poof!' He made a quick dart with his hand, dabbed at her sleeve, and drew his hand back. Quick as that. Emily taken by surprise, wasn't she just!

'Didn't see that coming, did you?' he said. Very solemn as he said it. Just showed you how quick a cat could be! A touch of amusement there too, Emily thought, when he saw her reaction.

God knows how they'd managed to make something like this between them, Barry her son-in-law, tall and pleased with himself, and Meg with her name on the side of the Lexus she drove and 'No 1 Sales' there beside it, which she pointed out to her mother, as though she couldn't read. 'When you consider the competition with the way the market is. Phew!' She moved her head when she said that, as though following a bullet.

Not a thing you'd say to a soul, but even your own daughter could bore you. Meg and Barry together. 'A power couple'— wasn't that a phrase she had read somewhere? Business breakfasts. Festival concerts. 'I didn't know you liked modern dance, either of you,' Emily had said a month or so back, and Meg told her, 'The important thing with our sort of lifestyle, the calls made on us, is to keep Donald's feet on the ground.'

'As opposed to where?' Emily had asked.

'Mother!' Meg's mock frown of reprimand. 'Why do you think we just love it that he comes here every Friday after school? Eh?' She hugged her mother as she told her, 'Values. Do you think we want to end up with a spoiled brat? We see them all the time. I don't think you realise, Mum, how much we rely on you.'

His grandmother would say, when she presented the boy with the plate of freshly baked melting moments he loved, and the glass of Sprite, a drink that his mother said should be banned, for heaven's sake—didn't Emily appreciate the dental havoc sugar caused?—'Time for our values, Donald.' The boy smiling without answering, aware in some obscure way this was teasing his parents. Both of them.

Emily supposed the boy was clever. He mostly won their games not because she allowed him to, but through his knack of seeing chances on the board more quickly than she did. At other times, when he was bored with reading or playing in the mess of the garden, he sat up at the piano that no one had touched since Meg left home. He played a few simple things quite nicely. Played with feeling even, if she could say that without making the kind of claims that grandparents so easily fell to making. It wouldn't matter in any case if he didn't shine. As Meg had done. As the boy's father still liked to do. She guessed the boy liked spending time with her without having to live up to anything. There were afternoons when she wondered if his occasional listlessness had to do with his already understanding what his parents expected of him. His just sitting there some days in the big armchair, looking out to the grey light beneath the roof-high hedge, the torpor of waiting being rather nice in fact. Not that Emily could really know about what a boy that age might think. They liked each other, that was what mattered. Liked to be in the house with just the two of them.

'You look the way an owl looks when it's watching for

mice,' Emily told him, 'when you watch the board like that.'

Donald flapped one hand loosely at her. 'Perhaps I am,' he said. Neither needing to smile because it was just them. They both liked it when they shared a joke and neither had to laugh.

Then, 'That's your mother now,' Emily said. The sound of tyres on the gravel in the drive.

She had to admit Barry was right about that, when he said a year back that when you lived alone a gravel drive could be as good as an alarm. The next week the truck and the workmen were there and there it was, spread and crunchy when you walked on it, in time for Mother's Day.

The boy began to collect the pieces and arrange them in their box. 'You won't have time to beat me again,' she said.

'You never know, Emily. You might have won—if we'd finished.'

'Probably right,' she said. 'I was feeling lucky.'

Donald looked at her. 'I was humouring you,' he said. 'Mum said I'm good at that.'

'I don't think you do,' Emily told him. The slightest bit hurt.

'I told her we don't have to try about anything.' The boy chattering on, liking it that he could tell his grandmother something he knew his mother hadn't meant him to.

Meg was calling from the kitchen. 'Can you get a move on, Donny, you know Dad likes us being on time.'

'I know, I know,' the boy said quietly. He packed his few things together quickly, neatly. He kissed Emily on her cheek, touching her shoulder as he reached towards her.

'Come again,' she said lightly.

'As if,' he said. Imitating someone he had heard say that.

They walked through to the kitchen where Meg stood

ready to leave. 'One of these days I'll be on time,' she joked, ran her hand across the side of her hair, said, 'Another week like this and I'm out!'

The boy waving from the car, and the quick beep on the horn as Meg raised her eyebrows and puckered her mouth, her frantic Friday face.

Emily locked the back door and drew the bolt that had been there since her own parents' time. Barry had reminded her, twice in just the past few weeks, to make sure she was 'barricaded in' the minute she was there by herself.

There'd been a distinct demographic shift, he explained to her. Prices may have been leap-frogging but clientele, especially this side of the motorway, had changed. Was changing all the time. As if he were instructing a child on how the world out there was a big unknown. He told her just take a look next time she was out driving. 'Amazing,' he said, 'once you pay attention.' If only she'd sold up a couple of years back when he first suggested it. The tide creeps and you hardly notice and then it's caught up with you. Next thing, the break-in and vandalism quotient has suddenly escalated. 'You'd still do well if you decided to up sticks, Em. It's not the neighbourhood you and Alan used to live in. Not that I'm judgemental either but it's a thing to be aware of.'

It amused her that it was Barry who fired the real estate bullets. Meg presumably thought it wasn't her place to lean on her own mother, beyond her saying once, 'If you ever did decide on moving, mind you, you'd do pretty well.' How considerately, Emily thought, my flesh and blood put things! 'When your fucking number's up', as her own father would bluntly have phrased it. An educated man, her own mother had said, but the tongue on him! It's the army, she had said, trying to defend him. You don't go to a war and come back without some damage done. As if he gave a damn how he put things, as long as he was back, but her mother hated it. Language, as she called it.

Emily went back into the lounge and sat in the chair Donald so liked, without switching on the tall lamp beside it. Now that she was thinking back, don't expect profundity! The turns life takes, she thought. Her mother was a snob for one reason and her daughter a snob for another. 'Mother', as she had insisted on being called once she and Deb were old enough to be aware that how one put things most certainly did matter. Words, Mother said, were little detonations that told you where boundaries lay. And now Meg the bracket on the other side. 'Schools do matter!', almost shouting it at her when they had argued about where Donny would have the chance—can't she see that?—to grow up with kids who had the same values. 'You want to bring politics into everything!'

'You want fences around life,' Emily had come back at her. 'That's another way of saying ghetto.'

As if things had ever been so different. As if generations don't repeat themselves over and over. She thought of her own mother's obsession with drawing that big bolt each night, her removing the key from the lock above it and reaching up to place it on the high mantelpiece. There was always someone to keep out. She remembered the war when she was a child and her father had been away, and her mother would say if the Japs ever get here, we'll know about it then all right. Rice paddies as far as Taupō.

Next morning when she woke the room was chilly and the curtains still not drawn. Alan wouldn't have liked to know she was careless about that. The little changes before you noticed, as he liked to say. You have to watch these things, Em. His own problems already setting in, but neither had yet become alert to them. She walked through to the kitchen. The red glare on the bench where her daughter had placed the poinsettia, a thank you for having Donald after school. A different little gift each week. 'No one takes you for granted, Mum.' Ugly damned things they are, however much you crack them up. Those broad, rough dog-tongue leaves. Americans apparently couldn't do without every home having one at Christmas. She could see Meg in one of her rushes, braking in the New World car park, dashing into the floral arrangements section, declaring 'That one's perfect!' to the woman at the counter, no, no need to wrap it, truly. God, just look at her watch, as if she needed this as well! 'She wouldn't mind,' Donald said to her, 'if you didn't bring something—Em says that every week.' As if we wouldn't, his mother telling him.

She took the plant and its green plastic saucer and placed it on the old plush cloth that covered the oval table that had been there, with that very cover, since she was a child, since before the house became hers and Alan's. The years she had sat at it, reading, sewing, just running her hand back and forth across the dark plush, its faded brocade border falling at the table's sides. She glanced at the calendar above the alcove where the phone sat in a little blue plastic armchair. Meg's presents didn't draw the line at kitsch. The next time the boy was here would be the week before Easter, so no doubt an Easter egg the size of a pumpkin would be the gift of the week. Easter itself of course Donald and his parents would be across in Sydney. My God, as Meg would laugh, if ever there was my kind of town! There would be a card with the Easter egg that said, as her cards often did, 'What would we do without you?!!!' Too early to say, Emily had thought.

Criminal, she thought, the way prices kept jumping week by week, as she took the pinot gris from the fridge. It wasn't as if Meg hadn't said to her, and Barry too, for God's sake, Mother, there's no need to stint with anything. As if they'd see her measuring out Villa Maria when there were cartons, as Barry teased her, cartons of Te Mata if she'd swallow her pride. What I'd prefer, she had thought, really prefer, if I had any say in it, is that you were a different person, Barry, entirely. Or that I was, for as long as I had to listen to you.

Young Donald. Strange how the boy was on her mind so much. He made her think of a fledging perched on the rim of a nest. His school blazer with its pointy bishop's hat, its Latin motto with expensive words such as 'victus' and 'aurum'. All that boys aspire to because they're told to, all we reprimand ourselves for not quite achieving. Amazing, Emily though, the clarity that arrives at the end of the second glass!

She ran her hand over the faded plush she had stroked for as long as she remembered. Her mother, too, with a cloth not so very different from this one. Her fingers pressed for a moment at the hem of thick brocade. She recalled the game with her fat small hands as a child—how she'd hated that word fat when anyone else said it—lying across her mother's fingers which were so much longer and nicer than her own, with her rings that didn't come off unless she put soap on her fingers first. But then why would she want to? she said. Ever want to take them off?

Emily liked to think of the past because you could not mess around with it. You could not be sentimental about something set hard as stone. This is what it was, the stones said: you can walk among them if you like but you'll never change a thing. She disliked the way some of her friends spoke of years back as though it were some great chunk of blancmange, where you dipped your spoon and tasted just what you wanted to taste. You couldn't alter a thing: that is what she liked about it. Memory was Stonehenge from a choice of angles. It was there and you were here. You could look at it as long as you liked and imagine it looked back, but the terms were implacable. You took it for what it was, or not at all. The exhilaration, if you had the nerve to face it, of knowing exactly what you were. We know when we're tarting it up, putting a spin on things. But once we get it straight—it's where we sit in judgement on ourselves. It's not always so bad.

Her mother with her gift for fantasy, for her children always brighter in her mind than they were in anyone else's, her saying, refusing to say alcohol, to blame the piss, as her husband frankly did: 'The War of course was what came between us.' Unable to bring herself to say that they were never suited, before the war was even thought of. Mother's fingers stroking the table, year after year. Where Emily too had laid her head, forty years ago and more, her cheek against the flatness of the table, her own body too drunk to move except with effort, yet her mind cold and clear and merciless, the night after her abortion, the gift of refusing to excuse herself, whatever. The solace and disgust of drunkenness, the first and only time in her life. The relief and the horror, because indeed there were both.

The summer after her mother had died and life was hers entirely, that too for the first time. Alan back from Vietnam. God knows how they had got over that. Alan in the army and her in love with him and yet marching, shouting, 'Troops out now!' at the American Embassy gates in Thorndon. But in love and knowing they could get over anything! Alan, who was mild and considerate and who ten years later she betrayed in this very kitchen, this same spread velvet cloth beneath her cheek, but this time sober and as unconfused as she had ever been. Her sister in another city, Meg with relatives, the girl's first holiday apart from her, on a farm at Taupiri. A year after her husband's mind had begun to slip while his body, for all you could tell by looking at it, as much the man as it had ever been, that of the man she had loved, and now feared to be with.

Look at the past, Emily reminded herself, so it has to look back. The evening when Deb's husband had picked her up from the Home, where Alan was past speaking for himself. Her sister out of town at one of her Zonta meetings, or whatever. Dan picking her up because her own car had packed up that afternoon. He had driven her home, and she had said, as she did so many times across the years, 'You must have a cup of tea, at least.' The irony of a phrase one does not forget. At least.

Emily removed the poinsettia from where Meg had placed it on the bench, with the card's inanely smiley face. She made a coffee at the gleaming machine Meg and Barry had given her the Christmas before. It hissed and blew like some kind of metal beast, but the coffee was worth it. As good as the advertising promised. Can't imagine life without one of these, Barry had said to her. Nor could she, a few months later, that was the joke of it. She took the big red Avezza mug back to the table. Without noticing it at first, her hand back to its stroking, the nap slightly resisting one way, flowing with the brush of her skin the other. Her own hand. Her mother's.

As she supposed she had done, that evening. 'Hits the spot,' Dan had said, taking the tea from her. He had put his keyring, attached to its blob of Baltic amber the size of a bumblebee, beside the fern with its wire-thin extensions, its tiny leaves. Her mother too had kept ferns like that on the table for years. Emily supposed she persisted with them because of that. She did not in fact greatly care for them, their fussy delicacy, their air of pay-me-attention, above the hammered copper pot they stood in, the one thing her father lugged back from Cairo. Dan's keys chinking against the metal as he let them fall.

He sat there, Dan her brother-in-law, laughing at something she must have said, and then his leaning back, eyes closed, his head against the wall behind him.

'When's Deb back then?' she asked him. Trying not to convey condescension as she thought of her sister in Wellington for her Helena Rubinstein makeup course, some new scheme for selling not quite door to door, but beyond the confines of department stores and their redolent counters and young bright assistants. Her sister later explained to her how the visiting Australian representative's newsletter sensibly pointed out that women with the time and energy to care about their appearance would prefer to speak with another grown-up, and not in the glare of a shop, for heaven's sake! So that's where she was. Receiving tasteful advice in discreet surroundings.

'Back tomorrow,' Dan said. 'Late.'

Then everything happening within seconds, as she thought of it later, yet that could not quite have been so. As if life had become the sudden whirl of a washing machine. As if there was any rational way to think of it, speak of it, that was not a cliché, a banality, a way of excusing where even the word excuse could claim no place.

She had sat at the table, Dan on the small settee facing her, relaxed, talking politics, which he seldom did at home, dipping gingernuts into his tea. They enjoyed chatting together. She knew he would want a second cup. She went through to the kitchen to flick the switch. She saw him raise the sleeve of his jacket and check his watch. Always it had been like this between them, since Deb had first brought him home, tall and considerate, and her parents falling for him as they never had done for Alan, 'holding their counsel', in one of her father's slightly pompous phrases, about a man who served in the army as a job. Dan had been nice to her, the older sister, in those years of obsession, as Emily always thought it, when he 'danced attendance'—her mother's phrase, that one—on Deb, who accepted it as her due. Vapid, chattering Deb. So that was what romance was like! As her father used to say, in those early days, it was as good as going to the movies just to see them playing at lovers. Odd that she was thinking of that now, as Dan kept talking across from where she sat. She thought of Alan's rather unkind amusement when 'the colours began to fade', Dan absorbed in his travel business, long before Deb in her gift for advising the mature woman.

She had turned on the kitchen radio before returning with the fresh tea.

Something nice, please, she thought as she set the volume to a pleasant background level. Something baroque came through, calming and moderato. Formal and patterned and light, a kind of benign brocade. Her mind oddly noting such things, as she thought too how strange, as if she and Dan hadn't known each other for decades, and yet this feeling as though she must keep a stranger entertained.

'That's nice,' Dan said.

'Dreadful how we so use music for background,' she said. 'I have it on the YC station most of the time. Then ask me at the end of the day what I've listened to and I doubt I could tell you even one piece.'

'Filling in time,' Dan said. 'When it comes down to it, that's what most of our lives are about.'

His surprising her, saying that.

'Well, tea helps, to be profound about it.' She placed the cup and saucer on a low table beside him. Her hair brushed against him as she leaned forward, and quickly drew back.

'You're right there,' Dan said. Each of them taking refuge, Emily would later think, in whatever cliché came to hand. He was talking about his recent visit to the capital. The bad name it had for weather, and so deserved.

Crossing back to the table she saw how the plush cover had ruckled up on the far side. Like her mother in that too, she supposed, her liking things to stay tidy, stay smooth, the little habits that keep us going. She leaned across, settling the cloth ahead of her with her arms at full stretch, her heels slipping up from her flat shoes as she pressed forward against the table's edge, her calves taut with the rise. For a second there her body arcing forward, a diver ready to take off.

A mistake, as she would think of it later. No point looking for reasons, yet how one's mind goes over things! Her fingers fitting the cloth back down between the table and the wall, her knuckles against the chalky brush of the wallpaper, when she felt the hands set against the outside of her thighs, the coolness of the air against her suddenly exposed skin as her skirt was raised. Roughly? Gently? She had no idea. Knowing only she had been driven forward, her face turned and her cheek against the cloth's smoothness, the irrational and even demented fact—so it would come to seem—that this was not a surprise, still less an assault. A muddle that was never quite to be untangled. I let it happen and neither then nor now do I know if I regret it. Her bare feet now planted level on the floor. Her pressing back against him. To comply. As though

44

it were a fragment of time from other lives, but not their own. She would have no real notion of what he thought, of whether her brother-in-law, who deceived her sister, might feel guilt or elation or indifference—how does one presume to guess? Momentary. Beyond the vagueness of that, what certainty, even in herself?

The absurdity of it, that too, the grotesque and comic sprawl they would have seen had a film later revealed it to them, the copper pot of maidenhair fern rocking in its clay saucer, the plant's bouncing droop like a green claw dabbing down on her head, the rasp of Dan's breath and the sustained lurching of the table, and beyond that the silence that was there across them, like a canopy, the word that stayed with her, and the unlikeliness—what did this have to do with either of them? The bruise from his impacting belt against her rump. And no memory, even a week later, of what might have been said, or if they spoke at all, as they then put themselves together—what a phrase! Drawing themselves back to where the world, to call it that, had been ten minutes before.

It was several months until she saw her brother-in-law again, at her father's funeral. Dan stood beside his wife and his arm lay beneath hers as she stooped to take up a clutch of earth and lean forward to release it into the grave. Then the banal but piercing shimmer, as it always struck her, of the bugle at the end of the prayers, and the undertaker deftly removing the flag from the coffin before it was lowered. Stagey, moving, as it always was. Emily stood with a group of relatives and friends. Mostly old people. Younger than she was now, as she thought of it, her fingers beside the box where the boy so neatly stacked away the red and black pieces of their game.

These splinters, she thought, these fragments of history,

of what is really oneself. Yet almost everything a little trivial across time, which perhaps is what perspective comes to mean. If you looked closely at the faded cloth her hand returned to you could make out that once its pattern had been globed nectarines and sprays of curving leaves, although you would hardly guess at them now. How once they must have been.

'What's making you laugh?' Donald asked her. Their usual Friday evening. Their eating the omelette she always made for him and then the things cleared away and the pieces set out on the board, their clatter together as they poured from the box, clack-clacking on each other. 'You're always doing that. Laughing at me.'

'The way you think every game you can beat me,' Emily said. 'I don't know why you don't just give up.'

He knew she was teasing him. He didn't mind but sometimes he wished she would see he only beat her because he was getting better at it every week. He wished too that Mum would lay off thinking she had to remind him to watch his manners, to remember his grandmother was old and not to tire her, that you had to be nice to them, old people.

'I like going there.' He had told her that enough, you'd think she'd know. 'Of course you do,' his father would say. 'Like Fergus likes being put in his crate when we all go out.'

'Give it a rest,' his mother was likely to say when his father said things like that. Sometimes when they picked him up later on they wouldn't say a word until they were home. Then talking too loudly downstairs and Mum making sure his bedroom door was closed. He wouldn't mind being at Emily's a lot more than just Friday nights, as if he hadn't told them that. Of course other Fridays it wasn't like that at all. They would laugh and all when they got back home, they'd put music on, you'd think it was a party if you can say a party with just two people.

These last few weeks Donald had been on about the war, the one a hundred years ago. They had gone from school in a bus to see an exhibition. Guns, he told Emily, old trucks and things, an aeroplane made out of cardboard and stuff. Real blood, it looked like real blood on the make-believe faces and that. Like really dead. The teacher and another man explained things. Why the kings were fighting, although each country had its own special word for king. 'And you couldn't get out of it,' Donald told her. 'You just had to go because your country needed you.' He liked coming back to the planes. 'Did you know they only had stuff on the wings like, you know, stuff. Canvas or something?'

'I know, they were a bit like boxes,' Emily told him. She scooped the pieces together. 'You set the pieces this time so I can beat you again.'

'And if you dropped a bomb you just leaned over like this,' the boy said, leaning out from the table, ready to drop one on the carpet. 'You just let it go.'

Meg had warned her there'd be little else but war talk. She had no idea, her daughter said, why they so hammered the whole damned business of it even with the tiny kids. To think there were years of it before the bloody commemorations were over!

Then Emily suddenly remembered them. She knew Meg would be enraged. She went through to the bedroom and opened the top drawer of the tallboy, where Alan had kept his cheque book and passport and odds and end. It was pretty much as he had left it. She took the two medals from the box he had never removed them from. Surprising how heavy they were, and how fresh, how brightly their ribbons flared in the light from above the table. 'You might as well wear these,' she said, 'while you try to win against me.' And then, 'They were Granddad's.'

The boy was beside himself. His fingers ran across the crinkled material of the ribbons and the patterns on the cast metal discs. She helped him pin them on his school jersey.

He played now with a new seriousness, and Emily guessed what was in his mind, as he hesitated, revised his move, clicked with his tongue as his tanks moved across the board to annihilate her own. And after their engagements were over, she told him, 'I don't think you should take them home, they're so easy to lose. Although they're really yours. I'll just keep them here for you until you're older.'

'When you're dead?' Donald said.

Emily liked to think how his mother would have spoken in that tiresome instructive way of hers when instilling the kind of things you must and mustn't say if you wanted people to like you. 'And we want people to like us, don't we?', the flourish she tended to conclude with.

'Sooner than that. Once you're old enough.'

She guessed the boy was calculating his chances.

Then, 'What did they do,' he asked her, jumping back to tactical matters, 'after things were bombed?'

'Made them over again, I suppose. Put the lost things back.'

'To look the same?'

'If they could.'

'So a room like this would stay the same?'

'Pretty much.'

Strange, how saying something so simple moved her. She put one hand across the other, to hold it still, while Donald set up the pieces for what would be their last game before the lights swept across the windows as the car drove up, and his mother would fling in at the door, telling him to get a move on, you know how Dad hates waiting.

'I'm black this time,' he said. He tapped one of the pieces on the board, to warn her he was ready. His fingers came up and touched the medals.

'This time you're for it, Emily,' he said. The severe voice he used with her when there were still games to win. 'I mean, really for it.' He moved the first of his pieces forward to where her own, more threatening than ever, were lined up and waiting.

'Not a chance,' she told him.

KO TĒNEI, KO TĒNĀ

I

Quercus Park is not the most favoured part of its county, if you have progressive agriculture in mind, nor the most social, should hunts and gentry house parties come into your definition. But a reasonably fine prospect is commanded from the amusing turret erected no more than thirty years ago in a stand of ancient oaks. The Tower, as the family consider it, is out of keeping with the handsome stone of the two-century-old house. Those with nothing more than quick curiosity might glimpse the recent folly as they pass the high stone wall of the estate's western boundary. They may puzzle at what rises above the oaks, the legacy of the present baronet's eccentric father. For 'Mad Sir Jack' had exhausted his failing ingenuity on its forty-foot-high brickwork, its four raised corners shaped to replicate the stems of sugarcane, mingled with the overreaching foliage of palm trees, all worked from now discoloured limestone. For this, the Tower declared, was the seat of a man who had done well in the plantations of the West Indies, where his slaves, he boasted, were treated as if part of his family, while sweetening the lives of his fellow Englishmen at home. A sad irony, that Sir Jack died of natural causes, within months of the Act of Parliament that punished such men of enterprise, and washed England's hands of tolerating slavery.

And so Sir Jack's clever and reclusive son, taking up such privileges as his father had bequeathed him, committed himself to the sciences at which he had so excelled in Cambridge. Now in his middle years, he contentedly lived in what he called 'our little menagerie'. By which he meant the gathering of five who most evenings dined together, with so little formality, in a panelled room with its dull portraits of forbears the younger generation seldom raised its eyes to acknowledge.

Oliver's social notions, quite apart from his intellectual remoteness, would have placed him at odds with his equals for fifty miles. There was a cook, and a local man who filled other roles, from serving at table to grooming for the small stable kept on the estate. Oliver and his friend, the urbane Dr Osmond, referred to Godwin and Wollstonecraft and Thomas Paine, heroes of their student days, as familiarly as they did to Fothergill Cooke or Wheatstone. During the years when his thinking was given mainly to electricity, Oliver corresponded with and indeed met the great Faraday. They had spent an afternoon discussing the induction principle, and the closed-core electric transformer. But the humanities also held his interest. He admired enormously the younger Wordsworth, as much as he detested the curmudgeonly Tory who alas still lived. But above all he was a man of science. In recent years Quercus Park had been webbed with copper wires. 'Speaking threads', he called them, anticipating what he hoped would be his achievement, his belief that electrical impulses and the human voice might be brought together. He safely spoke of his ambition with Osmond. Other acquaintances might, kindly enough, think him deranged. Although apart from his greyish discoloured teeth—the result of sensual indiscretion which Osmond treated with mercury—Oliver was not a man easily disturbed. At times it bothered him, but not intensely, that his younger brother was not quite a gentleman, and without capacities one could point to. Possibly a wastrel, but Sir Jack's plantations, which neither brother had any inclination to manage, kept Quercus Park afloat. Their managers, of course, were Englishmen, while its workers were now men as free, you might say, as a Scot.

At twenty, it seemed not to bother Mason that he had nothing of Oliver's gifts, and no consuming interest beyond himself. They sat together in the study, which was as much a workshop as a library. Various metal objects, large and small, were set seemingly at random, and a bench held flasks, tubes, and a brass wheel that once started continued to turn under its own impetus, driving a series of smaller cogs. Other moving parts connected to a device whose glass tube could glow with agitated gas. Oliver happily explained why this was so, but failed to hold Mason's attention for more than a few minutes. Even perpetual motion proved too tiresome for the younger brother to comprehend. A dead frog, ticking with what seemed signs of restored vitalism when a wire was held against it, bored him too much to ask about. For a moment Oliver was tempted to gift Mason the sensation of an applied current, and then regretted the thought. Instead, he sat cleaning beneath his nails with the point of a Mercator compass as he quizzed his sibling. Each found the conversation tiresome, although for different reasons. They spoke a little about finances, inheritance, the need for even those whom the French so rightly designate *les gens fortunes* to find something worthy of their time, their duty even. Mason admitted that, to be direct about it, there was no profession he was drawn to, nothing, actually, that he could see holding his interest for a year or two, let alone a lifetime.

Oliver found it difficult to hold his patience. 'Elizabeth is younger than you, Mason, and without the schooling that so favoured you. Yet in some areas of learning she knows almost as much as I. She works with me on my projects not as an assistant but as an equal. Her gift for calculation already surpasses mine.'

Mason laughed, as though he were the one indulging Oliver. 'Then how fortunate she arrived here when she did. As it was becoming apparent that she might be useful to you as I should never be.'

Oliver threw the compass he toyed with on the papers in front of him.

'Marcus Aurelius,' Mason began. He was about to offer a quotation on calm and equanimity.

'For Christ's sake, boy!' Oliver's face reddened as it seldom did. 'I could buy you a commission with the simplest note to a friend in Whitehall! Service would *thrash* you into something.'

'Nothing I care to consider,' Mason said. He enjoyed the quick returns on truculence.

His brother altered tack. Oliver prided himself on a rational mind. His anger abated as if it were no more than a matter of turning down the flame on a burner. 'There must surely be something, Mason, that is all I am saying, something that interests you for longer than a fortnight? Something in yourself to elevate?'

And Mason, with as much sincerity as he could muster, held his brother's eye. 'What I want, Oliver, is adventure.'

'Adventure?' A word, he could tell, that startled his gifted brother.

'Discovery, then. You of all people should know the magnetism of that.'

A long pause, as Oliver considered that perhaps, after all, he did not do his brother justice. He folded his hands and asked, as a cleric, say, might enquire in an Austen novel, 'Of what, exactly?'

'Myself,' Mason said. 'To know the boundaries of myself. Of what I might be capable of, for good or bad. That is what each of us should be saying, Oliver. There is nothing in life we might know as we do ourselves. To know exactly what we are. The limit of life is the limit of ourselves. To know what our boundaries are.' And another pause, before he said, 'You must understand me now?'

Oliver looked again to his hands. He accepted there was nothing he might say to such a statement. He thought, we are no more brothers than are elks and dolphins. But what he said was simply, 'Shall we leave it there?'

Yet the gatherings for dinner were always congenial. The two women and the three men who ate together each evening gave every sign of being at ease with each other, their conversations variously domestic, learned, amusing, informed by the London papers Dr Osmond received every second day, and so politics and even social gossip were part of their evening fare. The occasional dinner guests—usually scientific persons of some eminence—would leave, gratified and surprised by the confidence with which the women spoke, the good humour that defined the table, the quite natural intermingling of simple family accord, and a level of discourse that was unlikely to be rivalled within an afternoon's ride in any direction. Apart from the fact that the monarch's health was never drunk, nothing was likely to strike a guest as untoward. Although on reflection, slivers of memory might well come together, and a number of questions raise themselves.

Of the marvellously impressive Elizabeth—Lizzie as the family call her—foremost, naturally. The rumours were rife enough of the tall, dark-complexioned young woman. As she entered the room she seemed, as one guest thought it, like the sudden striking of a gong. No one was unaware of her for a moment, however long the evening might be, or the pauses between her remarks. What the blunt might have called the sexual exchange between English males in the Indies and female slaves on the plantations was too delicate a matter to be spoken of openly when ladies were present. Yet it was not uncommon, God knows, for even the finest families to host 'wards', sent back home from those parts of the globe in whose climate, as Byron's verse reminds us, the very word 'sultry' finds its darkly obvious rhyme. But where nothing is said, all things seem possible. The baronet and his brother treated Lizzie with the easy courtesy they might a relative, shall we say. She and Oliver's wife Isabella seemed as close as confiding girls, as well as mature women. As one of the younger Huxleys—once a contemporary of Oliver's on a staircase overlooking the Cam, and as given to new knowledge as the rest of his distinguished family—wryly enough remarked, 'Whoever else might be guests at Quercus Park, Mad Sir Jack still haunts the table.'

As with any group of humans, the studious calm of Oliver's estate flowed above deeper currents. Oliver himself, with that signalling of symptoms at each partly concealed smile, had now of course settled to a more placid married life. Placid, although the word demands qualifying. Bella was the frankest, the least sanctimonious of women. With the assumed hopes for children so patently ruled out by her husband's condition, the couple admirably refused to take that as *final*, so to speak. On such matters they were unconfined by church teaching, or the commonly assumed English sense of decorum. As a tribute it might seem to Thomas Rowlandson, the great and amusingly shameless artist of moral and sensual excess, Bella and Oliver had refined a marital game named after him. Not that Oliver in the least was a man of excess. But occasionally he might ask, as if enquiring of something of no more importance than a mislaid hat, would his wife mind should Mr Rowlandson call that evening? And so the lurid depictions of art, the fantasies of an infamously proscribed novel from the previous century, Bella good-naturedly acted out. As Oliver, in his own curious selection of clothes, or lack of them, found the kind of satisfactions that might seem trivial or perverse to persons not sharing his own preferences.

Of the others who gathered to dine together each evening, less might be said. Whatever emotional promptings Lizzie harboured none might guess at. With her startling and marvellously springing halo of tightly curled hair, which ran with threads and tints of bronze when lit by candlelight, she seemed as removed from mere sensuality as did an Italian devotional image. While added to that her formidable gifts, her intellectual grasp of the work she shared with Oliver, and it was apparent enough that most men who came her way were in awe of her. Yet in conversation she was so amiable, so reserved. As Dr Osmond thought, but without admitting as much, she was one of the few persons he had met who was, at the last, impenetrable to him. Which could mean, could it not, that what so puzzled them was her simplicity beneath all else. Do we not always assume that if a woman is beautiful, and then clever as well, there is a greater mystery than may be the case?

Dr Osmond made such observations in a notebook he carried always with him, as those men are likely to do who believe each passing *aperçu* too valuable to risk its loss. As he had written for example the word 'volcanic', after examining young Mason several years back, when the fourteen-year-old boy was recovering from a fever. It was a minor enough event, but one that at the time startled him, and proved itself a harbinger, might one say, of the years between then and now. Minor, but enough for him to mention it to Oliver, who had seemed to take a more tolerant, less moral slant. The boy stood in his nightshirt in front of Dr Osmond, his head level with the doctor's shoulders. He had grown surprisingly in those last few months, 'outgrowing his strength', as was sometimes said of youths who suffered from mild symptoms.

'Raise what you are wearing,' Dr Osmond had asked. His tone conveyed that, familiar as they might be to each other, this was a professional exchange. This was doctor and patient. Mason bunched his nightshirt beneath his chin so that it seemed curiously like the rufflings one sees at the throat of cathedral choir boys. But Osmond then struck by the paradox that forced itself upon him. He himself felt the prickling of embarrassment, which the boy quite obviously did not. His shock—for it was no less than that—as he took in the boy's 'moral disposition' as no other had yet done. Mason held his gaze with a sense of command, defying him to look elsewhere. For his naked body ticked with a raw insistent excitement. He had moved the ground from medical distance to a covert, indecent display. His upper lip raised slightly, showing the edge of his teeth, their resting on the scarlet tip of his tongue. His now a blatant challenge that Dr Osmond lower his eyes.

'The boy will take careful surveillance,' the doctor had said that evening. The two friends taking as usual their after dinner brandy in the scientist's study.

'It may be a stage he is passing through,' Oliver said.

'A stage that may last a lifetime.'

'I expect it was mischief rather than indecency. You know how intractable he can be.'

'A word one uses of horses,' Dr Osmond said. 'It does not do for men.'

As Oliver dredged up the old Latin tag of nothing human being beyond our sympathy, his friend sharply noted that the way educated men hid behind the barricades of Latin at times disgusted him. It was out-and-out evasion. 'It is the way a peasant crouches behind shrubbery to relieve himself.'

'Well, here's to shrubbery,' Oliver said, both men laughing, raising to each other the dull glow of their glasses.

They had agreed, up to a point, that Cambridge might do wonders for Mason, as it had for each of them. The rough-hewn timber the great university took in, that left as polished Chippendale. Oliver laughed again at his friend's extravagant comparison.

'We may be the last generation to claim such luxuries,' he said. 'God knows where our radicalism will one day lead the likes of us, Osmond. Privilege trimmed back. The vote extended. Women offered the same freedoms as ourselves. Fine as it may be in so much, the future will have less need for the great Dr Arnolds than we might think.'

'First God, then Rugby School!' Dr Osmond said. 'So what have we left?'

'Science,' Oliver said. 'That, not Empire, is what those like ourselves will offer.'

The two men had sat in silence for several minutes. Oliver touched a small controlling lever at the side of his chair. There was a click, then the soft metallic running of a chain. On the other side of the room, a bucket tilted above the red coals of the fire, and fresh clumps replenished it. Such gadgetry amused him. He considered, but quickly put the thought aside, how much it would mean to have a son about the house, to entertain and instruct in such simple demonstrations of motion, gravity, transference of energy. The thought brought him back to his marvellous good fortune of having Lizzie's precise assistance wherever his experimenting led him. Yet if such a gift in her, why so little of it in his brother? It troubled him, the thought that what paternity might pass on so meagrely to one appeared so fulsomely in another. From where then, might her intellect come?

So a story moves on several years, as simply as beginning a new line. Mason's academic terms in the rising mists of the famous fens, in the springtime of youth exposed to those more clever than himself, to the constant presence of young men who thought deeply of what existence might mean, what social duty entails. How knowledge is the privilege, as one of Mason's great teachers put it, of passing on Promethean fire, a thought in fact that made as little impression on him as if such things were discussed in another room, and he heard them dimly.

The brothers walked the estate together and chatted on Oliver's recent successes, the pinnacle being his election to the Royal Society, with Faraday himself proposing him. He conveyed the news as if it meant rather less to him than it did, but was hurt when Mason accepted it as if it were admirable enough but scarcely the crowning honour that it was. The boy is unchanged, his brother thought. His surface has been burnished, but little else has altered. They spoke of Mason's future. The young man said airily, 'Oh, the future, Oliver, it will come whatever we do about it.'

Oliver recalled, so long ago as it now seemed, that day they had sat at his desk and the teenager said to him, with such scouring frankness, that what he wanted from life was to press the borders of what his temperament demanded. He rejected, as if Oliver joked, the suggestion that he might travel to the West Indies, to the island the family still owned. The plantations had become all but a burden with their mismanagement. What an opportunity to prove himself, Oliver said. The opportunity, too, to show perhaps a gift for commerce? What Sir Jack had left them might enrich the family yet again.

'And do the work that slaves once did for us?' Mason said.

He said as much again at dinner that evening, with the awkwardness you might think of doing so with Lizzie facing him. But he smiled at her as he spoke, knowing she would feel the sting of it. Her loveliness provoked him, as much almost as the shame, which Oliver so absurdly seemed never to feel, of how close they might be in blood. When Bella too asked what he might do with his life, now that he was so equipped to face it, he surprised them all—the women who watched him with a certain feline alertness, the two men who presumed to think of themselves as exemplars. He said, 'I have decided on the furthest bounds of where Englishness counts for something.'

Almost a sneer, was it, in the words he spoke? Bella could not be sure. She tried her best for Oliver's sake to interpret them more kindly. Mason's attempt, she thought, to impress us all. Detestable as he might be. She felt for Lizzie's hand beneath the table, its lovely smoothness. Its barely perceptible pressure against the entwining of her fingers. She supposed it must still be in his mind at times, as she half intended it to be. The morning on one of his vacations between terms, when he had come into her room without knocking. It was a lapse of attention, an accident, which he knew at once his sister-in-law could only take as deliberate.

It had been a perfect August morning. She sat naked on the side of her bed, in the pouring of sunlight through the high window facing east. He stood with his hand on the broad doorknob, about to mutter an apology and withdraw. In thinking of it afterwards, Bella herself was uncertain why, instead of turning from him with a curt command, she not only stood but faced him. Mason's pulse raced with the brute fact of her provocation. It was as though she stood edged in flame against the shock of light behind her. The dark aureoles of her breasts as large as pennies. The taste of metal flooded his saliva. He stepped quickly back and left the room, clicking the door behind him. He rested his forehead against its cold hard panelling. Had she tested him? Made mock of him? He felt a deep rage against her. One day. One day there would be a reckoning, she might be assured of that.

And now he was on the eve of leaving them all. Dr Osmond spoke smoothly and proposed a toast. To whatever good fortune might come his way. Mason held Lizzie's eye across the rim of his raised glass. His returned words were cordial. He said he well knew what advantages life at Quercus Park had given him. The utter importance to him of each of those who so kindly shared this moment with him now.

'Then you must bring us something special,' Lizzie said, 'on your return.' Smiling broadly at him as she seldom did.

'Oh, I shall,' Mason said. 'I shall.'

II

From his first stepping to the wharf at the end of a street that rose to the crest of a low hill, Mason felt the attraction of his country's furthest possession. It was the main street he would quickly become familiar with, as he would with the lanes and side streets that ran from it. After the purity of the Gulf he had just sailed through, the views of forested ridges from the deck as he came closer to land, the distant beaches, the clotting of huts of what he supposed were the natives, he felt the exhilaration as the ship he had lived on for two tedious months swung into what the captain announced, with a kind of pride, as the Inner Harbour.

Imagine, the captain invited, what all this might become, with the energy and expansiveness the colony already so displays? But what came to attract the new arrival far more was what he did not speak of. It was the rawness and uncertainty of the new town that so excited him, the more so as he became acquainted with its canvas and timber huddle, the parodic business structures, the stage-set churches, the drive and naked self-interest of those he spoke with. His own mind curiously elated by its abrasiveness, the town's pretence already to be so much more than it was. Its edgy impression of peace, with the military casually present morning and night.

Mason watched the natives as closely as he did his fellow Britons. He accepted there was a wall between them that he naturally could not scale. Yet their distance, their frankness on one level and what he took to be curt indifference on another, drew him in ways he could not define. So that in his letters home he would speak blandly enough of their enterprise as part of the town's economy, the ferocity of their art and even personal appearance, that concealed so much more than it offered to view. He did not report how it was his sense of encroaching chaos, the loss of his own identity, that he felt at times, especially in the grog shops, in the illicit bordellos, in the swirling fumes and stink of places he found himself in, that so appalled, delighted. There was no way to write of such things, even had he wished. To please the two women who would be interested in his observations rather more than Oliver or Osmond, he wrote of the working-class females who still spoke as if at home yet already had taken on an independence that so readily crossed into presumption. But they—Lizzie and Bella—would be diverted, as indeed he was himself, by the fine English dresses, the close-buttoned bodices, the finely needled skirts they might expect women of some refinement to wear, the manners so carefully kept up in the salons (!) of the officer and business classes, the attention paid to fashion, 'even at this distance, and, as you would expect, not quite in season'. And the social pinnacle— where else, but at the governor's charming enough residence, where the replica of such events at home was well done yet slightly comic too. 'It takes so little in society to lapse, for the fault quickly to seem irreparable,' he wrote. 'Still, the pantomime keeps up with spirit enough.' Mason knew the women at Quercus Park would read past his irony to their shared contempt for 'standards'. His telling them as much. 'There is a good deal here that I believe you might enjoy.'

Yet so much more he did not convey. The depravity, for

example, that was not to be spoken of openly. An officer, well taken with the wine so generously laid on as Government House celebrated the anniversary of the young Queen's coronation, asked frankly, had he observed the way a native's eyes rolled back *in flagrante*, the merest strip of mother-of-pearl between fluttering lids? He spoke of the shadowed lives in the huts and grog shops along the downtown lanes, the scrim palaces of forgetfulness and delight, once the darkness came down. The respectable capital went about its lawful business a matter of minutes away. The lights of the deserving shone distantly from what, within years, would be the finer reaches of the city, along the ridges that ran like the rim of a bowl above the seafront.

Late at night, Mason liked to lie smoking a thin and expensive cigar in the rooms he rented on one of the town's eastern slopes. His own forays into business went well for him almost instantly, his partner a serious Methodist, a member of perhaps the only religious sect one could entirely trust. Almost nonchalantly, he invested handsome capital in an enterprise his partner would manage in all its details—the bringing across of farming equipment from Sydney, the kind of thing that new settlers had such need for. Once the governor had settled the problem of natives who for the moment wrangled about the purchase of land, 'the fruit was there for the picking', as he enjoyed informing Oliver. Some evenings he spent an hour or two in the Gentlemen's Reading Room, which a London agency provided for a small subscription. But he preferred to talk with persons of all stations, discovering a gift for penetrating character that surprised him. He felt that almost weekly, he became aware of aspects of himself that may never have surfaced had he remained at home. He quickly assessed how language serves to conceal more than it reveals; that clever men may also carry a lifetime of naivete, the way an illiterate, beneath what may seem a repellent shell, is capable of subtlety and intuition. He wished Lizzie were here to speak of such things. He missed the sharpness of her mind, even as his troubling lust for her blazed at times so that he loathed her for the game she played with him. Yet appearance too, like language, he thought. How it wraps, conceals, the core of what we are. How many layers must one be willing to divest, before one's essence is arrived at?

After six months in this still new and yet familiar place, Mason seemed at home in whatever company he kept. He had a good head for drink, and with means enough to be acceptable wherever a few flung coins might earn a man an instant loyalty, or half an hour's quick obliging. The governor himself was taken with his charm, his education, his connections in a county where distant relatives of his own resided. The two men talked horses, and the bookish administrator liked his quickness in picking up his literary tabs. Thanks to his half attending to his brother, he bluffed convincingly enough in his offhand talk of the sciences, and could say, quite truthfully, that yes, he had dined with Lyell. He was the kind of young adventurer a new colony so needs.

An American friend, 'stranded', as he put it, between changing berths, and hoping soon to travel north to sign on for a whaler travelling back to New Bedford, taught him simple card tricks, but not so simple they were known in the capital. The profit Mason drew from them was not the point, so much as the delight to be taken from the sleek fleecing of the naive. How far would he go, he thought, with a quickening that itself was a pleasure. How far might a man dare to reach his own boundaries? The elation of escaping the snares that convention throws at one? He knew one boundary at least was touched, when he heard how a nervous middle-aged man he had played with the previous evening had shattered dawn at Freeman's Bay with a gunshot that woke the street.

Another friend, a German who traded liquor and ran various semi-legal businesses, was the man he felt closest to, the one who to any eye but Mason's was the furthest imaginable from his own cultivated demeanour. Gruber's left ear was no more than a bulb of flesh. His chest was scored as though a bear had swept its claws across it. Yet he spoke quietly, even in the late-night clamour of his grog shop. He looked at whomever he talked to with what most men might consider candour, but Mason knew instinctively was something so much colder, calculating. It was the German who told him the details of the practice. Who picked up at once on the thrill that coursed through his English friend as he spoke of it.

It was a rare spell without customers as they stood at the counter beneath the dim inverted V of the roof. The rain that pelted in one of its quick passing squalls compelled them to speak more loudly than either customarily did. Not that it was an occasion for extended speech. Gruber unfolded three pieces of paper on the bar's long slab of kauri. Each displayed similar yet distinctly different patterns, the kinds of curves and swirls familiar to him from the faces he noted each day in the street, that seemed to him of all he saw in the colony, the deepest intricacy of what he failed to comprehend. His explaining how one must be patient, patient and careful, as the administration was severe in such matters. But their very rareness sharpened with some men the desire to risk the law. Gruber understood how Mason was already snared with the very thought of it, that the Englishman's will had frayed, as if an addict.

It was two days' sailing, in a scow of the kind built for what could be challenging seas, yet pliable in the shallow inlets as it travelled north, the tidal creeks with their mudflats and mangrove swamps. A young native called Matthew, handsome and polite and the product of some zealous mission school, adroitly managed the craft while its heavy built captain, with his peaked cap and his boasting of naval service, sat in the small cabin with his single passenger. He spoke kindly of his deckhand, who kept the craft's brass polished to a mirror, kept its tackle trim. The boy scanned the sky and horizon as if there were not a minute without a call for vigilance. Mason feigned a passing illness to escape the captain's torrent of reminiscence, his commentary on the coast they sailed off yet always kept in sight.

Several figures were waiting on the frail wharf after Matthew steered the craft up a narrowing creek. The wet banks glistened mud. The young man joked with those who had come from missions and remote solitary farms. Some came onboard to help with unloading the sacks, the bales, the dozen sheep, the lengths of dressed timber, the heavy metal blades for a flour mill. A tall man with a broad-brimmed hat waited to greet Mason as he stepped to the wharf, although 'greeted' is too fulsome a word for the curt nod he gave him, without offering his hand. The man referred to by Gruber, as well as the captain, as 'the trader'.

The visitor was led to horses beyond the wharf. A native, already in the saddle of his own mount, stayed at some distance, a rifle slung across his back. The trader said, 'You can be back here in two hours. Once you've made your choice.'

Mason attempted frank good-fellowship. 'Supposing I buy,' he laughed.

'You'll buy,' the trader said. There was nothing more to say.

In twenty minutes the track opened to roughly knocked-together stockyards, enclosing half a dozen cattle. Much of the land on the slope beyond had been cleared of bush, the grass as lush as the meadows on the estate's tenanted farms at home. From a wooden house with a veranda running its length, two women—one English, he supposed, one native—watched the men arrive. His mind was thrown back again to the two women at Quercus Park. They dominated his thinking, even here, in this weirdly pressing landscape, the pulse of strangeness he felt following the trader through what he had been here long enough to think of as 'bush'. Its dark pull towards whatever it was it might conceal, so distant from the earth's other side, with its landscape so timidly packaged, so exposed to certainty.

The men halted in the stink of the cattle yard, yet the odour still there, fragrant and foreign, from the tunnel of trees they had just emerged from. Perhaps because of the slim, silent women twenty yards off, the vivid image came back at him of an evening shortly before he had left. A small gathering in the drawing room after dinner, a scientist whom his brother so respected reading aloud from Shelley's verse. Mason had thought, 'What elevated rot.' But the small group hushed with reverence.

It was the instant he knew, beyond doubt, that he and Lizzie were not only of the one flesh but capable of a deeper bond as well. From opposite sides of the room they had held each other's gaze, while Dr Osmond pressed one knuckle again a leaking eye. While even Oliver, pragmatist that he was, sat with his chin supported on his joined hands, attending to the poet's 'ethereal beings'. Mason felt the glow of so desiring her, the tall, graceful woman with her tightly curled hair, the richness of her colouring. The *hauteur* which none who met her failed to remark upon. The slight swell of her breast beneath her bodice. A boy's body, almost, which so drew his will towards her.

But memory, with its random startling threads, was hauled back sharply to the moment as the trader too dismounted, tossing his reins to a youth who grinned up at the stranger. He led Mason to a stone shed without windows, not much larger than a prison cell. The trader lit a lamp, worked the wick so it flared higher, steadied, so that the small space was brightly lit. A long table was stacked with boxes and packages, piled papers, folded fabrics, and beside it the squat heaviness of a small printing machine. The trader cleared a space and said, 'I will give you time to make your choice.' Mason raised the first of the muslin-wrapped parcels the trader brought from a curtained alcove in a corner of the room.

It seemed no time had passed before the men were riding back into the green, diminished light of the bush. There was the echoing shot of a rifle to let him know the captain was intending to depart in thirty minutes. The tide had lowered the scow several feet. The sleek mud banks were more exposed, the scabbed spindled stems of the mangroves inches above the dark slurp of the broad creek. But in his riding back an elation rose in Mason unlike anything he had known, the kind of thing, as he later thought, that he had once seen among the crazed farm workers and itinerants after Wesley himself had preached not a dozen miles from Quercus Park. It was a feeling of attainment, of touching some chord in himself that was now fulfilled. But from so unexpected a thing, from the tapping against his knee of the large flax kit tied to the front of his saddle, and inside that, wrapped in finer softened flax, the whole point of his being here—a human head.

III

His brother Oliver was absent when Mason arrived back. A note explained that he and Osmond were in London, which he was obliged to visit more frequently since his election to the Royal Society. He was there to attend a meeting where the guest speaker was a great geologist. But hoped to return within a day or so. He longed to see his brother, to observe the changes which must be inevitable, as he heavily joked, after 'more than a year among savages. Or was it all far more cosmopolitan than that?'

The women welcomed him with both the frankness and casual distance that had always marked their dealings together. Yet Lizzie and Bella suspecting, too, from the minute he was back in the large familiar house, its furnishings and pictures still carrying as ever the mark of Mad Sir Jack's freakish taste, that he was quickened, even more so as he again took in his sister-in-law's fullness, the younger woman's slender *hauteur*. After such absence, they struck him afresh with a brute sexual force he was unprepared for. That image from years before of Bella's turning to him in her nakedness, her seeming indifference as to whether he looked at her or turned to leave . . . Or the evening when Oliver's friend read the poet's verses, the air so charged with Lizzie's protracted boldness. Her staring back at him, while the poetry's beat seemed that of his own blood, its words lost completely in this other raging silence. Until he had been the first to lower his eyes. But all that was then, he assured himself. This was now.

This first evening back, without Oliver's good-natured but solemn heaviness, or Dr Osmond's tendency to share his education with all, there was a rare levity when the three met at dinner. Mason's was a more generous hand with burgundy than his brother's, and the women pressed him for details of the new colony. He told them he was rather unobservant on flora, fauna, the things he knew the menfolk would so quiz him on, and Bella smiled across at him, telling him thank heavens for that! He amused them with his sardonic chatter of social life, at least of its upper reaches, its playing at social gradation, its discretion on mankind's usual follies. He lowered his voice, and the women leaned slightly towards him. 'Even the governor,' he said. The handsome young Māori woman who was part of the vice-regal ménage, and Mr Grey's evident pleasure in 'refining' her. Mrs Grey's starchiness so making it clear that it was a tutelage she herself played little part in. He told them too of the lighter side of military life, the resentment some officers, and their wives especially, held that they must travel to the empire's furthest flagpole to forge a career. There were those, of course, even among the womenfolk, who took to the new country, who found ways to ascend, succeed, as would never have come their way had they remained on the lower rungs in their motherland. 'An unfortunate taste of freedom,' as one cleric had said of them, 'that one day may lead to political *fracas*, God forbid.'

Then what had never taken place at Quercus Park before. After the one servant, who had served at table and helped the cook and housekeeper in the kitchen, had left with the elderly woman for the short walk back to the village, Lizzie said simply, with the calmness of knowing how profoundly she violated the customs of the house, 'Time I think, don't you, for our mad father's rum?' Oliver had long refused to touch the bottles which had come from 'Sir Richard's island', that lay beneath decades of gathered dust in a corner of the cellar. 'I will fetch it,' she said.

Bella looked as though a physical shock had struck her. Even Mason, part of whose *sang froid* was to place himself beyond surprise, held back his impulse to call out, 'No, Lizzie, not now.' But the girl was gone. They heard the slamming of a door caught in the high wind that was rising across the park, then sat without speaking until she was back with them, holding a bottle at her side. A grey smear from a veil of cobwebs in the cellar lay across her shoulders like a shawl. As if one breaking of the house's customs had dispensed with others, and with a directness that took Mason back to one of the Fort Street drinking houses, Lizzie said, 'The glasses we have will do,' not bothering to cross to the cabinet where the small glasses called rummers had lain untouched for years.

Her defiance, her bravado, seemed to let so much convention off its leash. The three brimmed glasses tapped against one another. There was laughter and even a raucousness the dining room, with its sombre panels, its few stiff-figured paintings, had not previously known. The harsh dark liquor was a novelty for each of them; 'Our family blood,' as Lizzie said. As if she had waited since girlhood to mock them all. And a loosening too from whatever Oliver, and his friend Osmond, might consider good behaviour. The two women sang a moving Robert Burns song together, and then a more sentimental piece by Thomas Moore; the delight the music afforded them of wallowing in unearned tears.

'Now you!' they demanded, and Mason, in his fine enough

tenor, remembered the decent variants of things the sailors had sung on the voyage out, and again back home. Things that were rollicking and jolly. The women tapped their glasses in time on the dining table. They leaned towards each other, and Bella's hand moved so naturally across to stroke Lizzie's bodice, tampering with its laces to reveal the almost childish breast. Yet rather than hinting at depravity, there was now an air of extraordinary naturalness in the room. Mason touched his sister-in-law's cascading hair as he stood and said, 'The present I promised Lizzie, before I left. You remember that?'

'I remember everything,' she said.

'Give me long enough to fetch it.'

He was back in the trader's windowless stone storeroom, his hand shaking slightly as it rested on the long bench of thick-cut timber while the three shrouded heads were exposed for him. He recognised the patterns from the papers Gruber had unfolded for him. There was no sense of revulsion at what he looked down to, but a heavy curdling excitement. So *this* is what we have arrived at, the buying and selling of dead slaves! He had come to the boundary of what human experience permits. The heads were placed on folded sacking, each tilted slightly back so that when the trader raised the lamp he held, they seemed to be confronting him, the teeth of two of them exposed beneath the upper lips, the discoloured gums oddly prominent. The eyes of two were closed, but with one, slivers of some pale polished shell had been inserted, so a narrow sleeve of greyish-white showed through narrowed lids. He looked closely at the swirl and close incisions of the green scorings of the tattoos, covering the cheeks and foreheads of what the trader offered. Mason's forefinger touched the hardened cheeks. The hair, black and shining as if lacquered, was drawn back tightly and knotted at the crown. Its effect of dignity, for all that it may have been subjected to, struck him as perversely handsome. It was as if something thrummed in Mason's being, this standing beyond the bounds of what most men would consider decency. The head dragged at him with a magnetism he feared and welcomed.

He now carried it through from his bedroom to the dining room, surprised as he always was as he first lifted its compact weight. The candles on the polished table seemed to slur against the darkness. But the women had refilled the glasses with the tar-black alcohol. They stood arm in arm smiling at him, impatient. Bella had let down the glinting fineness of her hair. As he passed her he leaned to put his lips briefly against the warmth of her shoulder.

Mason placed the muslin-hooded gift at the centre of the table. 'I'm afraid you must share him,' he joked. He drew back the cloth so his gift was tilted towards them, the slightly wavering candlelight brushing a drift of mobile shadows across it. He watched intently how the women might receive it. Bella's breath caught in a gasp, one hand raised so the fingers were against her mouth. Her other hand became a clenched fist that she pressed against the table. But nothing, in the many times he had imagined Lizzie in the long voyage home, had come near to this. She smiled slightly as she leaned towards it, and then again stood erect. 'A fourth person,' she said, 'has come into the room.'

'We must drink to it,' Mason said. Her words had shaken him. 'Drink with respect.' The women raised their glasses, but only he emptied his in one prolonged gulping, as God knows he had seen often enough in the Auckland grog shops with the stink of their habitués. He felt that first reeling of the room as he placed his glass back down, the bleeding together of the candles as they slipped across his vision. He

77

felt for the first time the wiry springiness of Lizzie's hair as she leaned in front of him, tilting the bottle she offered him. For something less than a fraction, he was thinking—and yet that too can carry the significance of hours—their heads touched. It was difficult for his mind to hold reality in place. Yet a pulsing aura, was it, that press of such seeming clarity as he watched the dark glitter of the bottle set down, and Lizzie's hand come forward? The bodice Bella had tampered with now fallen to Lizzie's waist. Her forefinger traced lightly above the engraved lines on the face in front of her. She touched the raised upper lip, but again so lightly. And her voice so distant to Mason, now that he needed to grip the back of a chair, as the clarity of a few minutes before crumbled into flaking darkness. His final memory of the night, Lizzie turning towards him in her part nakedness, unperturbed that he might see her, and saying in a quiet voice, the voice of a child almost with its hint of wonder, 'His gums are purple. See?'

The race, then.

Since Elizabeth's first arrival at Quercus Park, she and the then teenaged Mason had loved to race what was called 'the course', the long rising stretch close to the walled boundary of the estate, the turn at the very upper limit of the park, to the ten-yard-wide descent through the forest, with its various by-paths where for the most part walkers must go singly. From angles and breaks in the trees, Sir Richard's folly rose up, then disappeared. It was there, before Oliver and Dr Osmond returned, that the women, without telling Mason, placed his gift in a small higher room, in a chest that carried still the fragrance of camphor. No one had used the room for years.

More respectful than Mason, they had swathed the gift in folds of white silk.

The drunken night of his return was not referred to the next day, nor the one after that. Only a note that was slipped beneath his bedroom door, before he woke with his head beating as if inside a gong. His sister-in-law's fine copperplate handwriting, signed with Lizzie's name as well: 'Last evening, dear Mason, was so much more than we expected.' Both women, by lunchtime, had returned to the warm but slightly distant manner that so defined them. Mason walked in the bronze air of the autumn oaks, wrote business letters to what he casually thought of as 'our colony', went over and over in his mind the stark details that persisted through the confused memory of his homecoming. No words came to him that held it accurately, its sexual weirdness, its *farouche* excess. He was glad when Lizzie put to him, on his third evening back, the proposal that they ride the next morning.

'The race?'

'Of course. This weather. Before the ground softens with the rains a tenant this morning told me are bound to be here next week.'

'I remember I beat you last time,' Mason smiled.

'The mare was almost lame.' They laughed together, as old friends. As family almost, Mason sardonically thought. Yet that barrier always, tissue thin, between them, remember as he might such times as the evening before he left. Shelley's flighty vagueness skimming the drawing room from where he sat to Lizzie on the other side, her returning his own scepticism with her steady gaze. As if they flipped flat stones towards each other across a river, a child's game, yet heavy as jewels with their erotic charge.

'This time,' Lizzie said, drawing him back to the race she

proposed, 'a new challenge for you. We ride upright as we gallop.'

He laughed again. 'Isn't that slightly irregular?'

'You mean you think you'd lose?'

'I never fear what isn't likely.'

'We finish where the two pines narrow the track to ten yards apart.'

'Elaborate planning,' Mason teased her.

'It needs to be a race worth winning,' she said.

The early sky next morning promised a perfect day. The lawns and branches drenched still with glinting webs and runnels of dew. The sun was not yet above the level of the trees. There was chill enough for the riders to be wearing scarves. Lizzie as always in leather jodhpurs, a tight black riding jacket, a matching beret slanted and held firm with marcasite pins across the spring of her hair. She handed down the thin riding crop she carried to Bella, who stood in her deep green travelling coat, telling her, 'Skill won't need this to bring us home.'

Bella would act as starter and judge. She walked twenty yards ahead of the two nervy and circling horses. When she dropped a white handkerchief the race would begin. It was a touch almost of levity, like the starting of children at a village picnic. Mason grinned at the women. So much fun, he thought, so much seriousness threading it as well. The best sort of game. And the thin edge of anger, the feeling that for all his knowledge of them, the women toyed with him. But with his extensive riding in the colony, he was so much finer a horseman than when he and Lizzie last took the course their mounts now leaped to. He let her quickly gain several lengths on him. He would give her confidence, and then draw it back. The hooves of her mare flung up clods towards him. The pounding of the horses pulsed as if his own. He saw the veins begin to stand on the dark gleaming neck his reins crossed on either side.

Yet when Mason made what he intended to be an advantage on her lead, Lizzie remained those few lengths in front of him. The distance between them had barely changed. He felt the awkwardness of continuing to ride upright, resisting the natural urge to lean forward as they picked up speed. Lizzie's perfectly poised back provoking him. It seemed no more than seconds to the swing of the course at the far end of the estate. His heels drummed at the flanks of his mare. He saw how the tall woman ahead of him gave no more indication of urging her horse, than of restraining it. That sense of exquisite unity when a rider attunes to the force that so finely carries her. His irritation now rising to the blur of anger, as it came to him he was not likely to gain on her, any more than she would be reeled in. They crossed the upper boundary of the park, past the last acres of the season's dying oaks, before the turn to the long sloping descent at whose end Bella, not more than the size of a nursery cut-out, stood to the side of one of the Norfolk pines, her arm already raised.

In the next hundred yards Lizzie allowed him to gain on her. It was difficult not to follow his instinct to crouch forward, defying the absurd conditions she had placed on the race. Mason was close enough now that he might reach out to touch the black jacket of her upright back. And then the rapid swirling of the next few seconds. Lizzie threw herself forward until her upper body was level with the horse's back, her cheek touching the massive swell and working of its shoulder. She turned so her face was visible to him for the first time. He saw the nacreous glint of the eyes no more than a few feet from his own glance. On the hollowed mahogany cheek he saw the whorl of its ink-stained design. Her lip was raised to display white teeth in their discoloured gums. He had time to take in that what rode beside him was the head he had chosen in the fetid windowless hut on the world's far side. Yet it was Lizzie too, her bent form skimming beneath the invisible stretch of razor-sharp copper wire that passed through Mason's throat as neatly as a cheesecutter cleaves through cheese.

Lizzie wheeled Rosebud so the mare stood panting close to Bella. Mason's head had bounced on the short autumn grass twenty yards further on from where the women watched, and rolled into a clump of furze. While Candida, startled by the sudden release of the reins, galloped on, the figure on its back tilting with what seemed unnatural slowness, before falling from its saddle, one booted foot caught in its stirrup, the rider dragged until the mare stopped abruptly, and the riding boot fell loose.

Lizzie's calculations had been exact. Bella tightened the wire's brace as she saw the horses curve at the crest of the hill, raising her hand to turn the screw attached to the side of the pine. Hadn't Oliver warned not to ride in the park without informing him? The wires that he believed would bring him fame, rigged in unexpected places. Dr Osmond confirmed how the death, you might say, was extraordinary, but quite explicable. He also insisted that the ladies not see the head, with its purplish contusions and its oddly regular lines etched across the forehead from the fall, before Mason was buried, with a brief and secular ceremony, within view of Sir Jack's Tower.

Should a wire be run, the women liked to say, from the removed and replaced panel they had attended to in the Tower's rarely visited upper room, a wire run down to what they referred to as Mason's mound, it was not impossible, with a little imagination, to project a conversation of sorts. But that was not a matter for today. With her sardonic turn of mind, Lizzie said, as she and Bella lay embracing together, she supposed it all depended on how successful a scientist Oliver might be.

Bella's tongue was licking at Lizzie's upper arm. She lightly circled the younger woman's breast, small but upright as a thimble.

'What was that?' Bella asked.

Lizzie told her again.

'Maybe more than that,' Bella said. Kissing her friend's full lips. 'More than that.' Unsure now what it was she may have meant. Each intent on the moment's vigorous demands.

THE YOUNG GIRL'S STORY

'Yes, yes,' Mandy said quietly as the voice called to her from the next room. She sat at the dressing table and held a long silver earring against her earlobe, turning it slightly as she viewed it in the mirror, then faced herself directly.

She called out, 'Yes, Cliff, I've spoken with her about it.'

She wished he wouldn't keep using that diminutive when he spoke of their daughter. 'Does the young girl really want to go?' Yes, of course she wanted to go. She was fifteen and could make up her own mind. Men could be so slow to see things. Didn't Cliff see that it would be an *adventure*?

Mandy placed the earring, with its threads of intertwining wire, on the dressing table in front of her. She took up a chunky piece of amber, a lovely deep honey gold as she raised it to the light by its slender hook. One of her grandmother's pieces. 'It shouts Baltic at you,' her sister would say. Meaning too rustic for words.

'Yes, I'm quite sure,' she called back again. Dear Cliff. He had become something of a museum piece himself. Their daughter happily teasing him about it too. His woolly jumpers. His leather elbow patches. 'You're so retro, Dad.'

Amber has such a life of its own, the way metal never does. The first time she met Kelvin Stein at a conference a few years back he had touched one of the earrings so gently she had shivered with embarrassment, as if he had brushed her skin. Before they became good professional friends. A kind man, whatever the rumours that some postgrads liked to hand about. He had come down from London for a weekend and he and Cliff hit it off famously. Kelvin liked telling him about his books, and all this kind of thing was new for her husband, who had no idea what to expect when a scholar came to stay. He knew it must be good for Mandy's career, and it had not been such an effort after all. The bottle of Bushmills Kelvin had brought with him of course had eased things along.

And now here they are, the likelihood even of a Manson edition she and Kelvin Stein will work on together. Not yet quite lined up but really as good as. Again, Cliff was the one to throw it into perspective, in his downbeat way. 'Every carpenter,' he said, 'can do with the best apprentice.' It would all be sorted out anyway at the conference. Although, Cliff took some convincing that it made sense for Mandy to take the young girl with her. Wouldn't she be bored stiff?

'It'll do wonders for her French.'

'So long as you're sure.'

It made not a jot of difference to anyone, Mandy thought, as she stood up from the dressing table, ran a brush quickly through her hair, and went through to join the family in the next room. But of course the amber were the thing.

She was beaming as she handed nuts around, with even Louise given a glass of Asti. It was one of the girl's weekends home from school. She looked up from her texting, happy to see her mother happy. It was only an hour since Mandy had stopped at Louise's bedroom door with the printed-out email in her hand. 'Dr Stein,' she said. She knew this was a special mother-daughter moment. 'Dr Stein has read my paper and says it's numero uno. After his plenary it will be the first one up.'

'Brilliant,' Louise had said. She now scooped a handful of

cashews and said, 'So what do you think of Mum's news, eh, Dad?'

'And that's not all,' Mandy said. Not minding in the least that her cheeks glowed with the excitement of one thing topping another.

'It *has* to be all,' Cliff laughed with her.

'The very next email,' she said, flapping the folded print-out against her thigh. 'I've been asked to speak on Manson on Radio 4!'

Louise smiled. She knew from hearing her mum say it often enough that young people used metaphor to excess, and she knew her comparison was a touch over the top. But she couldn't help it. Her mother really was like a jockey waiting to be hoisted up, tapping an anxious whip against her leg.

Mandy sometimes said, when Cliff wasn't there, just how much she and Louise owed to him. Once, he had worked fourteen hours straight at his computer. He stopped only once, for a bowl of spaghetti. Those Germans, she said, that he contracts to, do they expect their pound of flesh. Not that he minded in the least. He was devoted to them. When Mandy started a little later than most at university, he was with her every step of the way. When reading Manson knocked her like a thunderclap, never once did he ask why, but simply, 'How can I help?' As a boy from hardworking parents in the north, he knew what he thought politically, but social mobility scarcely bothered him. So for Mandy's sake, even more than Louise's, he went along with a private school for his daughter—a fine timbered mansion in an extensive park that was never listed as educationally top-drawer, but that drew, as the brochures insisted, on a wide spectrum of parents who realised how schooling of this type, which offered riding stables as well as art trips abroad, meant as much to girls from sound English homes as it did to the international catchment pool, whether Russian or Saudi.

Louise thought of the school as a movie set, with good manners and Anglicanism as marketed by Harrods. She made notes about it in *cahiers* as Manson may have done a hundred years back. She liked having a secret literary life her mother would never have guessed at. She quite knew how hard her father worked so that she and her mother might have the satisfaction of rising a few notches. She loved him for it. One day it would all pay off. He was the one of course who had first mentioned to her the chance to accompany her mother, as though it might have been his idea in the first place. Darling Dad. Because of a recent school trip to the Imperial War Museum in London, it was easy to think of how heroic he would have been in Ypres or one of those places. I'd be grateful if you'd allow me to go over the top with the first of them, sir. Louise could easily imagine him saying that.

And now it was back to the conference itself.

'But where do I come in exactly, though? Won't it cost a fortune?' She stood behind Cliff's chair, a hand on each of his shoulders. She gave her young girl's easy laugh. 'Not like Dad's a sheikh, is he?'

Mandy said, 'You know Daddy doesn't mind how hard he works if it's for our sake. Or your sake, pet.'

'I'm resigned to the workhouse,' Dad said.

Louise watched her mother flicking at the long string of beads falling across her cashmere top. How much grown-ups could tell you without saying a thing! She took her hands from her father's shoulders and sat in what they all jokingly called her homework spot, a puffy leather chair with a patterned

Greek cushion. She said her friend Francine, who was French and so ought to know, told her that people in that part of the country, in the south with its striped beach umbrellas and Italian waiters, all spoke English anyway. You'd learn as much French staying at home and watching a movie.

'That sounds clever but it isn't,' Mandy said.

'It could be true,' Cliff said. 'Francine ought to know.'

'It could not,' Mandy said. As if Cliff, who wasn't up to ordering a cold beer, would have the least idea!

'That's what Francine—'

'I think you're being ungracious about this, Louise.' Her mother had stopped her bead flicking. She always sat very still when she was serious. 'Your father makes this lovely offer and you simply don't seem to be very nice about it.'

'Dad knows I don't mean that.'

'But *I* don't know, do I, Louise? It would be nice for me too to know you're grateful.'

Cliff could see where things were heading. 'Well, let's make a life of it, shall we? Let's eat at the club.' He meant the Harrington, a desirable club one of the other mothers from Louise's school had her husband put them up for. Not at all what you'd think, Cliff joked, if you simply went on what you see in the car park. He meant its rows of top-end motors. But it had its own film theatre, a pool with the loveliest lighting so that at night it seemed the walls rocked with the purest pale blue reflections, a bonhomie, as Mandy said, that was a delight in itself. Always someone in the lounge to chat with, or—yes, she knew it sounded naff to say so!—to look at. All within twenty minutes' drive. When it snowed, especially, or in the full glory of summer, you were as likely as not to see photo shoots for good magazines.

At the airport Louise hugged her father and said, 'I still wish I didn't have to go.'

Cliff ran his hand across her hair. 'Things often turn out better than you expect.'

From the moment they touched down in Nice, and there were cries of recognition across the baggage belt, her mother was on a high, embracing friends from earlier conferences, making herself indispensable. Louise took them in, between her texting to Francine and Evvy, her Russian friend at school. She liked seeing Mandy so happy. She thought about Dad having to take care of himself, though now hours away in a dull Hampshire afternoon, while here *they* were, walking out into warmth that roved over you like a warm hand, and palm trees, and the glitter of the sea bright as shimmering glass. She would try to like it as much as she could. She laughed when she thought of her dad telling her, last thing, 'You're a lucky young girl,' so the moment they were on the coach that would take them along the coast, she'd sent him a text telling him, 'Yes I am. YG.'

Louise had not quite realised how much it meant to her mother that her daughter was turning out to be not just pretty, in that sudden sort of rushing way girls her age could be, but something rather more. *The real thing*, as Mandy had confided recently to one of her best friends, a Woolf expert with a monograph out this summer with Toronto University Press. She had said as much to Cliff, who took it rather lightly. Mothers tend to notice it first, as he said. But now, as if it had not occurred to her before, Louise was, within a few hours, aware of what her mum was up to, the almost too obvious look of satisfaction when her daughter was introduced to new people, as if it was Mandy herself being freshly admired. But she spoke as if it was for the girl's sake that she had travelled with her.

'It would have been too cruel,' Mandy said, 'to leave her at home in what we English laughingly call the summer, and deprive her of all this.'

A swarm of scholars from different countries were standing on the balcony of the restaurant hired for the conference's opening dinner. 'All this' was the sweep of the bay in front of them, the great rise of the pink cliffs behind them, the horizon, sharp as stretched wire, far out beyond the dotted yachts and billionaire launches. Right beneath, the golden scarf of the beach. At first the sound of talking was subdued, but voices rose as drinks were taken from passing trays, empty glasses replaced and fresh ones taken up. Quotes flashed about like darting birds. People made a point of coming up to speak with Mandy. Her amber earrings made the softest clinking as she moved from one to another, enthused by half a dozen conversations. Everyone seemed to know who she was. And then there he was, the famous scholar, talking to her, but careful to take in her tall, shy daughter as well. No, it's *Kelvin*, he was saying to Louise. Goodness, they were all friends here, no need to be formal.

Louise had heard so much of him it was inevitable that when he was there, within touching distance, he disappointed a little. The first thing she noticed was how his eyes were able to move very quickly without his having to turn his head. She thought he would make a good detective in a big store. She felt a little bit sorry for her mother when she said, almost immediately, that she was next thing to certain that she had solved the mystery of the McCarthy letter, and Kelvin said, kindly enough, oh, there would be time for all that in the next few days, as the Woolf lady drew him aside, saying something to him that made him smile. This drew back the skin of his cheeks so they crinkled like crêpe paper. It was a friendly smile but Louise imagined two little hooks drawing down the corners of his mouth, so it was an unsmile at the same time. Then there were more people milling around her mother and Mandy was introducing her and she felt again how they were looking at her, but not for her own sake, really. She felt as though she were something nice that her mother wore. It must have been a phrase she had come across in a story or somewhere—'the daughter as attribute'. It was not a feeling that she liked.

A bell sounded from down in the restaurant below the balcony. Everything looking so lovely in this late light, the way it slipped its warm gold across people's faces, across the falls of wisteria loading the iron rails. The space cleared and the crowd moved towards the staircase circling them to the floor below. Louise looked down on the descending heads. She heard Mandy's laugh coming up to her, and could have leaned across and touched Kelvin's head as he walked the curving stairs a little ahead of her. The top of his head she thought would have felt like paper too, yellowy and brittle, as men start to look when they are famous and elderly. Laughing to herself though at how silly it all seemed, thinking like this, unable to get *papery* out of her mind, now that it was there.

One glass of champagne that a kind woman had handed to her, and already feeling she was looking down on herself turning and turning, brushing against the stone wall, as the line flowed down in front of her. How tricky things could become, even to know what you were thinking inside yourself! But everyone, all these people as old as her mother or even older, seemed so friendly and happy together that

Louise was happy for them too. The things and people she had heard Mandy refer to at different times without actually listening, were suddenly here all around her, and they were *nice*. So this was Julie Bancroft from Somerville who was working on Beatrice Hastings, clever as a monkey so Kelvin was supposed to have said of her, and who was really pretty if you looked carefully at her, who was the one who had handed her the champagne and joked, Someone has to look after you! And the much more severe Paige Ryan, an American, who wrote reviews Mandy had said with a blowtorch rather than a pen, and looked scary enough, but had talked to her about her son who was the same age as Louise and would no more read fiction than she, Paige, was likely to play Grand Theft Auto.

Louise liked watching the conference people. Some so much quieter than others, some liking to laugh a lot so others would look towards them, shy Kyoko whom Mandy made a point of being so nice to, who would very likely ask her to be her supervisor once her grant was set in stone. She heard someone say it could be hard work drawing in Asian scholars at times, that carefully written lectures told you nothing actually about the difficulty with face-to-face conversations. You could tell too who were the important ones at the conference, you could feel it in the air. Louise tried to joke about it when she and Mandy were in their room after the first day. Her mother was lying on the bed with her eyes closed, her shoes shucked off, desperate she said for half an hour to herself. Louise said, 'You know, Mum, how dogs can pick up different kinds of traces at the same time? Like different scents? I reckon you could just about do that here. Who tries to be nice to someone, how someone else is sort of shaken off? Everyone clapping papers and then how they sit together or sit somewhere else afterwards?'

She thought her mother had not heard her, or had drifted into sleep. No wonder if she had, the energy she poured into everything, knowing everyone by name, chairing Kelvin's keynote so competently, clearly delighting in her own address, the way she dealt with the McCarthy letter and the Costello suicide in one of the stories, a crux if ever there was one.

But no, she hadn't nodded off. After what seemed a long time, Mandy said, without opening her eyes, 'That's not a generous way to think, Louise. It sounds like you're trying to be clever at other people's expense. You miss the whole point of occasions like this if that's how you think.'

Well, she'd be able to talk it out with Evvy, her Russian roommate, once she was back at Westing Grove. Evvy, who was great fun and said Pussy Riot were female Rasputins which was why she adored them. You could say anything to her and it was impossible to surprise her. She wished she could think of something that Evvy would even mildly admire her for. The first Russian word she had taught Louise was *mudak*. 'That is all you need to know about my parents.' Anything Louise could ever say about her own life seemed so tiny and clean.

'It was only what I thought,' Louise said, 'first off.'

'Then thinking again about anything's not a bad idea.'

A few minutes later Mandy said, in the nicest way, to show she wasn't put out as she may have sounded, 'You could always be a wonder and make your mum a cup of camomile.'

The girl saw of course the good things her mother had meant her to see. The way the women of different ages were friendly together, how the younger ones laughed and shook their hair out in an arc as they climbed from the pool. The way after the afternoon sessions people sat in groups and carried drinks from the bar and each table seemed a party, there was so much fun and calling out, and one table outdoing the other with called-out clever remarks. Manson might be an author who had been dead for a hundred years but you would almost think she was still there, the special friend of all of them. And behind it all the solid graft, she heard someone call it, the work that so went into articles and editions and teaching and the sheer hard yacker, as Dr Stein said in his plenary, using the casual language that the audience so responded to, theory-hater that he was. Though when he came to one of his sharp attacks on 'Derrida and Co', whatever that was, a few of the younger scholars laughed with the rest but were a touch uneasy. Not that Louise could possibly have been aware of that had Paige not pointed it out to her. She wondered if the American who had made rather a point of watching out for her felt as Mandy did about everything Kelvin said. 'The life of the mind, indeed,' she said, when Louise had lost the drift of things. But she had never seen her mother quite as she was at the conference, 'always on top of things', that was said so often of her, as she organised schedules for the Romanian conference next year, and signed up subscriptions to the *Manson Studies Annual*. It was only that afternoon when she closed her eyes and rested for half an hour that she was anything but on fire. Her mother was like that though. She could be down as quickly as she was up. Deflated so quickly. Louise heard her talking late that evening to a close friend, about another scholar who had come up with some vague notion for a publication of the kind she and Kelvin were almost certainly going to collaborate on. The woman, a busy little lecturer from Hull, had actually bailed her up and asked hadn't she a few professional qualms about it?

She must have known she herself had talked to OUP? As if anyone *owns* Manson!, Mandy had clawed back at her. Such a bitch, she was telling her friend. Louise pretended to be asleep when her mother came into the room. You could tell by the way she thumped at her suitcase, and slapped her folder on the small desk, that she was upset. She sat and opened her iPad and her fingers flew across the keys until she calmed down.

Louise, as it happened, spent a quieter last day than she or Mandy had imagined. In the morning, playing tennis with a nice fatherly man from Adelaide, she had turned her ankle so that it was simply too painful to walk on. One of the hotel staff kindly strapped it but already her foot was puffy. So much for the planned excursion then across the border, an Italian lunch, a drive high into the Alpes-Maritimes. Everyone admired how mature she was, a teenager after all, when she said, 'I'll be just as happy here with my foot up reading *Mansfield Park*.'

Mandy said, 'I'm proud of the way you're taking this, love.' But: 'Like fuck,' the young girl said to herself. She was supposed to finish the novel for her finals but would happily crib notes from one of her friends. If there was a Booker Prize for the most boring book ever written she knew where her vote would go. Did anyone ever bother to count how many times ladies drank cups of tea in Jane Austen? Heavenly Jesus, as her friend Evvy had taken to saying, so people might think her Irish rather than Russian.

The coach rounded the big circle of grass in front of the hotel. There were some who were choosing not to go on the excursion. Two Czech women everyone guessed were an item said they would loll about at the pool. The nice man from Adelaide needed to leave mid-afternoon for a flight. Dr Stein, who would lecture later in the week in Bordeaux, said he had two days to bone up on Apollinaire or the first-year students would catch him out. He could seem so droll when self-deprecating. Whatever he said, there was always someone who would smile at him. Academics, she thought. Like anyone else really, weren't they, into groupies, into wanting to smoodge up. Her mother desperate to play the game, to be in the top group. As indeed she was. The collaboration. Everyone knew about that by now. Well, wasn't it obvious she should be the one invited?

Louise did not half mind the chance to be by herself. Her mother said she could ring Evvy and another school friend at home to help pass the time. And Cliff even, if she felt like it, although any news they had could probably keep another day until they flew back.

Then, as it happened, the day could not have been more boring. Louise's foot hurt and her friends were not there when she rang them although it was not a school day and there was nothing to do but watch TV that was mostly in French and the only English language channel was the BBC World News. At least on Sports she found a women's soccer game, before a Grand Prix began and she switched off. Mum had walked the short distance to a patisserie and brought back a quiche for her to have for lunch, as the hotel assumed no one would be staying in. It tasted rubbery, for all the French went on about their cuisine.

Louise took a glass of wine from the bottle that Mandy had brought down with her. She had not realised she was tired until she woke and looked at her watch and it was past mid-afternoon. Her tongue felt dry and thick. She drank a tumbler of water and took two Panadol and limped towards the window to look down on the hotel grounds. The Czech Mates as someone had called them were no longer at the pool. A couple of elderly people sat on canvas deck-chairs. She felt suddenly quite angry, and didn't know why. But as she bunched the thin curtain into her fist then let it fall back to its set folds, she said aloud, 'This place pisses me off.' This place. The conference people out there on their excursion bus. The thought of her mother no doubt talking on and on, her amber earrings swinging as she turned, the Manson enthusiast to end them all. Another whole day until they were home. She picked up *Mansfield Park* from the table where it had lain since breakfast and hurled it at the wall. 'Pissed off,' she said again. It was all becoming so clear to her. Was it ever.

It would be half an hour or so before the excursion people would be back. 'Not after five,' the woman at the desk in the lobby told her. 'They are never back after five. Not with Antonio driving.' The woman smiling at her, yet at a distance in that way the French have when they are assisting you. Louise went back to the room and showered. It was difficult, wetting her hair while trying to hold her bandaged foot outside the fall of water. Her hair then dampening her shoulders as she sat out on the tiny balcony, her elbows spread on the ornamental iron ledge, her forehead resting on her hands. When she closed her eyes, pink dots chased each other behind her lids.

The plan was there as clearly as if she had written it down and learned it off. She had seen that Kelvin Stein was sitting on the lawn-level veranda of his ground-floor room, at a small table he had taken out into the fresh air, working there with an opened book, and a folder of papers, and a glass of beer. The big palms in front of the hotel were as still as if carved from whatever it was people dreamed about when they thought of the Riviera. The sun dazzling off the stretch of sea as though reflected from a knife blade.

Louise tried to make her limp less obvious as she crossed between the empty cane chairs and two big Pernod umbrellas and said in a way she knew was young and nice, 'Professors must never come to the end of their books. Or do they?'

'Well, there are nicer things than books, Louise,' Kelvin said, making a joke of being *gallant*. He pointed to a white plastic chair, the mate of the one he was sitting in. 'Shouldn't you be resting that foot of yours?' He asked would she care for something to drink? 'Something your mother would approve of?'

'Something not wine but in a wine glass,' she said.

Kelvin smiled at that as well. He repeated her order exactly to a waiter who had been standing beneath one of the palms, smoking a cigarette, bored with the world.

They were quiet until the glass of pale juice arrived. It was so easy to sit and say nothing when the afternoon seemed so still at this time of day, if you could put from mind the traffic that went one way along the street in front of the hotel, its flow of hot metal and fumes you could smell threaded with the scent of the flowers trailing from the balconies. *Glycine*, the waiter said, when she had asked what they were called.

Then: 'They should all be back anytime,' Kelvin said. His face so old when it simply rested. Sad even. Who knows what goes on when people are inside themselves? Books about books about books. And then life is nearly over. When he took off his white hat with its wide brim and little brass-rimmed holes at the side like portholes, she thought, I must make him look happy.

'Is it that late?' she said.

'Enough for the day,' he said. He tapped together the loose pages in front of him and she asked, straight out, 'Is that the book you are writing with my mother?'

'Editing together,' he corrected her. 'It's a long-term plan. No, this is something else.'

'Oh,' the girl said. 'I thought it was all, you know, set to go?'

Kelvin smiled. 'Your mother's a tiger for getting on with things.'

'Everyone says that.'

It was late already. Louise laughed to make Kelvin think, yes, he had got her mother *exactly* saying that, and pushed back her chair and went and stood behind his own. She surprised him, leaning across his shoulder with her long arm brushing against his. She must smell lovely, not the least embarrassed as she thought so, and remembered her mother saying to her before they left, before she herself had ever really thought about it, 'There won't be a person there who won't think you a dream.' Her knowing now, as precisely as if something sharp were pressing into her skin, what her mother had in mind all along. That she would charm old Stein, which could only help her cause. How few minutes it takes for a child to see the world for the first time.

She stirred with her fingers the few sheets of paper on the table, as if in some way she were teasing him. A kitten messing up his papers.

'That's the bus now,' the professor said. His voice distant, suddenly cold. Was he angry, even? She stood closer against his chair, its plastic curve pressing against her stomach. The big silver nose of the coach was entering the drive. The seconds slowing, and yet happening so quickly. She reached her left arm across Kelvin's other shoulder, so that hand too touched the papers as she leaned over him, laughing. The coach was pulling up and the faces from its windows were there like a row of plates on a shelf. Its front door swung out with a soft pneumatic hiss, and Mandy was the first one off. For those just arriving back it must have looked very strange. The professor there with the young girl draped across him, laughing, the empty glasses on the table, Dr Stein quickly standing, almost throwing the girl back with the suddenness of his rising, no one really knowing what was going on. His elderly man's cloth hat for watching cricket, jaunty on the girl's head.

Mandy pressed a tissue against her eyes for much of the flight back. She drank two brandies without asking Louise would she care for something herself. Cliff met them at the airport and they dropped the girl off at the big Victorian mansion that so made the school look solid and English, suppose an oligarch, or a sheik, were considering where a child might get the most from an education abroad.

'Don't even ask!' Mandy said, leaning in against Cliff's patient certainty. 'The bitch!' she said. 'The little bitch.'

Cliff stroked her arm and knew it was better to leave things until she was up to telling him more. However awful it might be.

They were back on the A4 before Mandy breathed deeply and rested her hand on his as it lowered to the gear lever. Was there anything that wasn't unravelled?

'It was worse,' she said, 'it was worse than those little sluts in Manson's stories!'

As Clive turned beneath the lovely arching of summer

trees onto the private road to where they rented what was called the Gate House, which God knows was more than they might sensibly afford, Mandy raised her hand to the sudden feeling of nakedness on her neck. She could not believe it. Things like this didn't happen. The amber earring simply wasn't there.

Was there anything fucking left to lose!

THE WALKERS

He knows some of the people who smile at him because he passes them so often, but he does not know all their names and they have not asked his so he does not smile back. Tommo though knows lots of people the proper way so would say hello and say this is my boy Eric and he would smile back himself. But not always now, because Tommo was not with him, so it was not the same.

Not the same but some things are the same. Things in the shops and the buildings and whatever don't move. But weather changes day by day. Only when they are put together what they do follows what weather has always done, what is different one day but not so different the next, and with a long time between them, rare days come round but not in order.

He and Tommo specially liked to walk on such days to see things that happened only then. One day in Bedford Street a tree lay across the road and one end had torn up its roots and bits of the ground still stuck to it. It had fallen across a fence that lay smashed up beneath it. Or one of the best days when he and Tommo had walked into town. In Hanover Street a crane crashed down its huge yellow arm and people in other streets must have heard it, and Would you believe it everyone said, there just happened to be no cars for it to hit and even the air they stood in jumped. They were on the corner near the red brick church and a man on the step called out it was a fucking miracle and Tommo said people like that didn't know how to talk nicely. Parade days were special. The day when a gun went off in the Octagon and the bagpipes people blew their cheeks out and pumped their arms and the men wore their kilts and it was the birthday of the big metal man who sat on his throne above all of them and wrote, Tommo said, famous songs. Exciting, Eric sometimes said. Exciting's right, Tommo told him. They squeezed each other's hands. But whatever, Dad said as well, walking's the story, eh cobber?

There is not a time when he can't remember Tommo. At first way back when he was so small Tommo had to bend down to talk to him, or when they had a car and he would sit in a high seat and his dad leaned across him to go *click* and make him safe. Eric thinks Dad in his head but nearly always called him Tommo. Must be times he can't remember that make him think now of turning the pages of a book one picture after another and then suddenly a page where there's nothing. Tommo said that was like forgetting, a picture there but just not on the page. And the pictures in your head that were yourself but you didn't mind if you forgot, because how would you know?

His time at the Best of Schools as people always said, where he was left for ages, but Tommo always coming to get him back for a while and then the Best of Schools again. No one was mean but it was a long time. He liked to stand at the window near his bed with his own rug that he had brought from home and his own locker for looking after things. Not to see the traffic on the road and the people walking past the fence of iron sticks on the other side of the gardens, but to watch how the sky along the top of the big hills was different one day from the next, and he knew where to look because another boy had told him, where to look for where the sun went down beside a high bit of rock, when it went down *there*, you knew summer was starting and school was over until next time. The best day ever of all at the Best of Schools when Tommo came to take him home forever. Because Eric's teacher said he was doing well and this was as good as it was going to get. It was three years now and by gosh (Eric remembered the teacher saying that) with time flying as it does, probably best to go home now. Tommo joked with him as he sometimes did with words and told him Can you imagine, Eric, you're a *tractable* boy, you must take after Dad. He had shown he could get on well with other boys but not quite at the stage where he wanted to play games with them but most certainly was not disruptive. Not in the least. Tommo told him other things they had said about him at the school. He was quick with numbers and could read beyond the level expected. But no, not real jobs you had to go to every day like you were a prisoner, but there were things at different times you could do at home, like helping the man who made paper poppies for people to wear on Anzac Day, and cutting up the branches of a palm tree into the right-sized pieces for the church the lady next door went to. And jigsaw puzzles, the teacher at the Best of Schools had said, he was a whizz at anything like that. Right things in their right places. He's a fortunate boy to have a dad like you, the Head complimented Tommo.

Home was at the top of a short sloping street that was called a Terrace. It was high above the harbour and across from the bigger hills on the other side and at night the lights of roads and houses poured across them down to the water that was a black sheet. Most nights the lights were still but on some they winked and flicked, it was a miracle, the word he knew was right for what he was looking at. Home was a brick house in the middle of not a street but a terrace. Suppose you were at the shop on Musselburgh Rise, you turned into Tainui Road then into Arawa Street and right into Aotea

Street and right again and that was the Terrace. But there was another way up if you were at the long stretch of grass in front of Bayfield School, and you crossed the road towards the left instead of the right. That way you walked along flat Bayfield Road and past nicer houses on the steeper bit until you turned to Aotea Street same as you did coming up the other way. A very different way again on those days when he and Tommo walked to St Clair and the Italian café with the shark bell you saw through the window no one was ever to touch unless a shark poked its way to the surf. Going home from there and looking up from Victoria Road you could see far away up on the hill the yellow house over the road from home, that way was past the Forbury Park Raceway Eric could see from the deck above the garage when the race track lit up on race nights and the shiny horses small as toys with the little carriages spinning behind them and the colour my gosh if he looked through the binoculars and from up here at home, right up here, the sound of the loudspeakers too he loved on nights like that. Anyway it was still a way walking back from there and the ocean you couldn't see but could hear on one side still and then Norman Street and Kamura Street and there you were at the other end of their Terrace, with two white lions on top of pillars made from blocks.

Eric and Tommo sat down some nights with a book that opened onto maps of all the places they walked, and it was fun to write down how far it was from this place to another, and how many hundreds of streets Eric knew and where exactly. Most days when they went walking they would decide on the Chinese Gardens say or the Stadium or the walkway along the rail tracks or wherever. And before they set out Eric would recite the streets that would take them there without looking at the map. Tommo made jokes about it. He said they should sell their telephone number to the taxi people so when a driver had no idea where to go he could ring it up and there'd be Eric ready to put him right. At the Chinese Gardens where the rocks made pictures in the water and it was always very quiet Tommo said you were meant to sit still so the quiet came inside you until you and everything else were like part of each other.

Sometimes maybe thirty people a day said hello to his dad, who stopped to talk with them but never long enough to stop their walking for long. Eric looks down while Tommo and a lady talk about her white dog that is the kind that pulls sledges along on ice, or the Indian man in the shop whose wife wears what looks like a flag wrapped round her and the dot between her eyes that makes him think of the head of a red nail. There is a man through the window of the Danish cake shop who always waves to them and the man outside Real Estate who stands in the doorway and smokes a cigarette because inside that isn't allowed. Eric will say some nights when they are having tea and before the people who know everything that happens come on television, Today Tommo twenty-two people said hello to you.

Hello to *us*.

Hello to me because I'm with you.

Because they know us both that's why.

Eric does not include those who nod sort of sideways or say Goin' there are we? Only those who say a sentence properly and Tommo answers back. Seems no time, some of them say, was only up to your shoulder I remember and look at him now, will you? And they do that, they look at him, and he starts to move away so Tommo will have to come along with him.

It is after breakfast most mornings when he decides. Tommo reads the newspaper and says if there is anything that might interest Eric, and the sports scores out loud. They both have teams they like and if Tommo says his team won 15–8 Eric will remind him last time it was his team who got 21–16 and the time before that, he knows the scores back to the start of the season.

But no, I wouldn't say we ever get bored, do we, Eric? If someone says Filling in time can't be so easy? Jesus, even, Tommo says, the way the days go. Eric feeding the birds first thing, filling the upside-down bottles with sugar water for the tuis and the bellbirds, pushing slabs of dripping into the red net bags onions come in and you can hang up for the waxeyes. Making jam. Cut-outs if it's too wet to walk. Planting once the spring comes. Always something. And cook. They always cook together, why wouldn't they? As his father says to the Ministry people when they come to check, but never where Eric might hear him, There's not much the boy can't do if he had to live here ever by himself. The people who carry the folders Tommo says that are always giving them ticks, the both of them. He says It's a bit the way streamers are put up for the rotary party at Christmas time, it's a way of saying This is a good place to be, only happy people allowed inside.

Then one day when they walked to Cumberland Street and sat in a room at the hospital until a lady said 'Mr Stevens' and looked at the people in the room until his dad stood up, and went with her to have an X-ray, Tommo said for the first time ever they would get a taxi home. This was because something happened that hardly ever did. It had been cold walking down from home though both of them were in their puffer jackets and wore beanies that were Otago colours. But now when it was nearly five o'clock and starting to get dark it had begun to snow. Suddenly white twisty ropes falling at them and the lights from cars picked out swathes of it and already it was lying across the plants outside the hospital and in just those few steps from the footpath to get into the taxi there was time for flakes to stay on your shoulders, and the swishers on the windscreen packed the snow in little ridges that made it hard for the driver to properly see. Then a push of wind and the snow swayed against the car, and you saw just the shapes of people like you looked at them through a curtain that kept sliding.

But Tommo was right for a few rounds yet, he said, if he did what the hospital told him to. Some days more and more, though, he would say, Might give our walk a miss if that's okay sport, but he still liked to go down to Forget-Me-Not, that was their favourite place of all to go together. Other people must have thought so too, but mostly they were able to have a table to themselves. When they stood at the counter Tommo would always say You go first there, eh, and Eric pointed at the bacon and egg slice. The lady who was usually Sonja turned the plate to find the biggest piece for him. It was a place he could time to the very minute how long it took to get there.

Tommo said he liked it too because people at other tables talked across and laughed and knew each other's names. How long was it I ask you Sonya, Dad said once, since there was a place as friendly as this in George Street? His dad always tapped the glass cabinet to where the cheese rolls were on their special plate and joked with Sonya and said if she didn't give him the best one straight off he'd just keep eating them until she did. Then while Tommo read the paper that was there for free, Eric looked through the big window as people went past leaning on those frame things that stopped them falling and more people had long beards than you'd see anywhere else, and ladies stopping to lean over babies in pushchairs to make sure they were wrapped up properly against the wind. South Dunedin Tommo said was something else again. He always dabbed at his cheese roll with his finger to make sure it was just the heat it ought to be. When he took his first bite he would roll his eyes at Eric and sometimes say to Sonya if she was looking, I'd do time for these know that? Not that Eric always understood him. Like when he said, his cheek pushed out with the roll he was eating, If you needed to bribe the Mafia sport you needn't go further than Forget-Me-Not.

Then Tommo was back at the hospital where they had been the day of the snow, back in the big building with one floor of beds on top of another and Eric sat and held his hand and his dad reminded him of things he might have to do by himself, but they both knew that, they had talked about it hadn't they, and it wasn't as if Tommo wouldn't be with him just in a different way, more watching than walking, think of it like that. And he said too, You know enough people by now, just about as many as I do. They'll always say hello. And anyway Sonya who lived not so far away would pop in, Eric knew he could rely on her as if she'd been an aunty.

I'd do everything like you do, Tommo.

I'd like that, Tommo said, more than anything.

It is good to be able to think that. He watches *Country Calendar* and the sports channel and plays their tapes like they've always done. He cooks nice things for himself and as Dad had said Sonya comes to see him and other friends of Tommo's and there, every day, were the walks, his knowing the way to take them better than anyone else in the city probably. Some days it's sad. Of course it will be, Tommo had said, but there are days too when thinking about Dad made him close nearly as he has ever been. And it was like he said as well, all the people who talked to Tommo say hello and are nice to him and mostly he says hello back and smiles at them and keeps walking. People don't need words all the time to be friends. Although time passes and the calendars are changed and different people come and go. There are still some who say things like a lady did once to another lady outside the Community Centre, Things seemed to work out all right there, didn't they?

They had never walked to the Bus Hub because it wasn't there back then, it was the ordinary street from the hospital up to Moray Place but now there are all these shelters to stand or sit in if you wait for buses that left for all the suburbs. At different hours there are so many people he avoids it, so many on the footpath you can't help bumping into them or they bump into you so all the time someone is saying sorry for it. But one afternoon he is there walking through from the Octagon to Countdown and pupils are pouring down from the schools up on the hills and there he is suddenly in this group of boys who look at him while he waits to get past them. One of the schoolboys who is tall as he is says Waiting for Wakari are you? Two of his friends laugh and one says Bet they don't know you escaped yet though, do they?

Eric says No because what they said wasn't true. But another of their friends who has a hood pulled up over his head says Of course he's from fucking Wakari, where else would he come from?

One of the boys bumps against him and says Oh, sorry there, dude, so the others laugh and they are blocking the pavement and people are having to move around them. The one with his hood up says, Christ, no wonder you're frightening the girls! He says that to make some schoolgirls in their uniforms laugh as well. Eric's neck and his cheeks grow hot and he tries hard to say the right thing. He says,

115

turning towards the girls, that he had been at the Best of Schools. His own voice sounds strange to him, like someone is holding his throat too tight.

The boys double over at the brilliance of it! The best of schools!

I'm pissing myself to death, the hood boy says. Did you hear him? Did you fucking hear him?

Somewhere from behind the circle that surrounds Eric a lady calls out, Leave him be, can't you?

The boys are dancing at the sheer fun of it. The taller one who started the game reaches up and snatches Eric's yellow and blue beanie. Go the Highlanders! He throws the woollen hat into the line-out. So many other people are looking now. What would Tommo want him to do?

He does not have to decide. A man who must be a tourist, you can tell by his skin and the way his eyes slope back, comes from the edge of the people pressing about all that was happening. The man moves quickly and grabs the boy's arm and pushes it up behind his back. The boy yelps and buckles forward until his knees are on the footpath, and the man telling him, Pick up hat. He moves his grasp so the boy yelps again. Pick up hat.

The stranger man takes the hat that is handed to him, and the boys and the people and the schoolgirls move away. He slaps it against his side so any dirt from the ground is shaken from it. He then hands it to Eric, who stands still as he takes it. He knows he must say something but does not know what. Nothing like this has ever happened to him. He knows it is right to say thank you, but that is not enough. He smiles at the man. As if Tommo is there beside him he remembers his often saying to him, If bad things happen Eric you will know the right thing to do. Good people always do.

He looks down on the head of the stranger, he sees the sweat between the black strands of hair. He holds in both his hands the beanie that has been given back to him. The man bows slightly and goes to turn.

Eric says, almost shouting, it is so important to say it. I can bring you a cheese roll.

THE FAR FIELD

Rachel, I decided, was the first I had to tell. She is the one I believe I know best, and she is the one who may have liked least what I had to say, the youngest, the one Grant made such a fuss of. She enjoyed that, knowing her father attended to her rather more than he did to the others. Part of Grant's little vanity was that he was too good a father, too careful a father, ever to show who might matter most to him. But Rachel knew in her bones about pecking order, so she was the one I would tell first.

Sometimes Grant would say, when I was content to sit and read, or when I spent hours in the garden or at the computer editing foreign students' essays for the polytech, 'It must drive you mad living with an extrovert.' Smiling as he said it, and I would smile back, our not needing to say more than that. Our knowing how it was one of the things that made our living together as contented as it was. His forging ahead, cutting the track. My waiting for the ready-made path.

How grateful I was for his doing well what I was so bad at. His easy way of finding things to say to strangers when we sat beside them at weddings, or stood balancing our cups and scones in church halls after funerals. I smiled and feigned interest and those we spoke to believed both, while Grant carried off the rest, the sympathetic memories, the quick amusing anecdotes, the right words where they needed to be. It never occurred to me really that I may have disappointed him, or just how much he did in keeping us all *afloat*.

I said that to Delia when she flew across in a break between productions, to help me with sorting her dad's papers. She was good at that kind of thing. How a sentence should be written, how pages are kept in order. And her saying, with a sharpness that surprised me, 'Like those bloody great lilies we were taken to look at in the greenhouse in the Domain? Special temperature. Special care. Just to keep it afloat.'

How much weight words can be made to bear. In tears herself once she saw that she had hurt me. Delia, the one who six months later—which can be the worst time, as you sometimes hear, for those who go into grief with such support and then find they must go on with it, alone—six months later phoned. This deal to Australia, she said. Return flights and a train trip from south to north, across the wide red heart. She rang not to ask if I would like to go, but to say it's all done, it's a goer, Mum. I just rang to tell you the dates when we can go.

I would say at times, after some particular kindness to me, or his doing something for all of us that I knew was an effort for him, 'You're my ringfence, Grant,' which became a joke between us. I can't think where I dredged the term from. Certainly from nothing I knew in my background. The dictionary did not define it quite as I expected. But we both knew exactly what it meant to us. It meant that when he would have preferred that I go along with him to some occasion, some special Rotary evening say, or one of the few times when he was talked into an event at his old school, he did not press me to go with him. Or when his sister phoned for his birthday, reminding him as she always did that there was a bed waiting for us should we ever be that far south, he would raise his eyebrows at me in the way that said, no, not that! Not Gloria's well-meaning local trips and endless variations on risotto.

Ringfencing was the word for what he did for me. Saving me the fraud of pretence. Years back, soon after we got together, he used to say, 'But that's what social life *is*, honey.' Or tell me, 'A few hours here and there that make the world go round?' But it got so I didn't have to say, 'Not my world, Grant,' and he knew I was grateful to him. Sometimes he would come into the tiny study where I sat at my desk, and I would feel the warmth of his breath as he placed his lips on my hair before heading off to one of his meetings, and he would say, 'I'll tell the lifeguards we're in this together.' I was grateful over and over again.

There is a woman, one of my son Jamie's patients, who tells him that her problem is that her husband so seldom lets her out. Of what, I ask him, why's she carrying on about that? He says she wants less love in her life, not more. 'I know what I'd tell her,' I say to Jamie. He looks at me with his good-humoured expression, which I guess means he's halfway towards being a decent doctor. 'Sometimes, Mum!' and he leaves it there. Thinking perhaps, as he looks at me, Well there's one woman it's too late to change.

God knows what Delia will say to me. But Rachel first. Then Jamie.

The younger two are still here, in the city where they were born. Although Rachel was off flatting the moment she turned eighteen. Grant was a little hurt, but said nothing. He insisted the children must be unconfined, be free to find their own way. Rachel was vital and popular and sang with the not very good bands her friends put together. But she worked hard at her degree and five years later was no firmer in what she wanted from life than when, as Grant used to say, she took on the world without us.

She tried a year at teaching and hated it, and then was working at Waitomo as a guide. Loving it. Taking tourists underground, getting them to hush so the glow-worms would come out for them, 'which they don't always do', then bringing the tourists to the surface unscathed, walking back to their bus. She and Jamie were thick as thieves. He teased her, yet also meant it, when he said how he admired her, the enjoyment she took from making strangers happy, and getting such lousy pay for it. And her mother teasing her as well, saying, Look at you, the first to leave home, and the one who is still closest to home. Rachel, who at times was frank to the point of embarrassment. Telling her grandmother at a family wedding, her grandmother who was troubled you could never tell these days how young people felt about things, that she liked men all right, Gran needn't worry about that, but she didn't want to own one so long as there was one to borrow from time to time. I thought, she is the one who will like it least, when I have to tell her.

Rachel was born soon after we came back, then Jamie eighteen months later. Delia was already two. My pregnancy the reason why we returned, to the city so commonly thought of by our friends as drear reliable old Waikato. Where Grant and I went to school together, to the same small university together. Grant a year older, talkative, a touch bossy, and by our early twenties each of us approved of by the other's family. His were farmers out from Cambridge, very into bloodstock but happily drew the line at testing humans. No one minded too much that mine went back to a railway house in Frankton. So we did what so many others did at the time. Worked picking fruit near Corinth, took office jobs in London, deciding after Delia and a year in Scotland that the Waikato might indeed be what the hymnbook had in mind as 'the green hill far away'. Those long months as 'caretakers' for a once wealthy estate north of Aberdeen survives in my mind as keeping Delia cough-free in a dismal rambling house, and spending as much time in bed as possible, the cheapest way to keep warm. Grant remembered that too, years later, when he took ill.

'By gosh,' he would say, 'we didn't half make the most of it, did we, up there in the Arctic?'

Something naïve, touching, in his wonder harking back to it. He was too shy a man to say such things had he been well. Besotted, I suppose. We both were. Jamie called in late most afternoons, checking, as I strangely thought of it to myself, on what no longer could be checked. And after our son had left and we sat in the descending evening light, Grant with his pillows stacked behind him, that was the time he liked to talk, to raise the past as best he might, until there was quiet, and after a few minutes, I knew he slept.

There was a night he came back to, several times, when we had sat with the fruit trees just coming out a few yards beyond his bedroom window. 'The night, remember that? So cold we sat with the eiderdown wrapped round us and sipping at the scotch until it was finished.'

'Ah, yes,' I would tell him. 'How could we not remember?' The night Rachel came from.

His talking out the memory of it. The flat expanse between the house and the distant row of trees, and the pyre, twice the height of a man, some local children had been assembling for months. Earlier in the day, a tap at the kitchen door, and a child hidden away inside her padded coat told us shyly they would be setting it alight that night, we must be sure to watch. And not to be afraid. Their fathers would be with them.

We had sat huddled and sipping with the lights out, watching through the window. Dark figures ran about the leaping flames. We heard the hight excitement of the children, the calls of the grown-ups. We had no notion of whether there was purpose to the great fire. Some deep memory, was it, appointing this the night for it to be lit? We were outside anything it might mean. Later, as the fire sank, it glared on through the darkness like a slowly tiring eye. There was singing that drifted towards us and away. We had no understanding of why the bonfire excited us as it did. So many years later, as Rachel leaned across him, and he wound a length of her hair around one finger, 'My bonfire girl,' his telling her, and Jamie and Delia thinking his mind was wandering, as it had been a little those last two days.

I held his hand, looking at how his hair had thinned. His eyes would return to mine, then glance away, with that same pale green colouring as the girls'. There was the afternoon when, through the big plate glass of the lounge in front of us, we watched Jamie step from behind the wheel of his Lexus, and his friend Seng from the other side. Our son's hand ran along the flank of the car, a touch of boyish pride. The wind suddenly lifted his summer collar, taking me for a moment to the way it had been the modish thing when he was at school to wear one's footy collar raised up at the back. Grant said, as he had more than once, 'I wish his friend wouldn't keep bringing me books. He knows I only flip at them.'

I said, 'It's because Seng wants you to like him.'

'As a sort of daughter-in-law?' Grant smiled at how sardonic he must still sound. He had come a long way since Jamie first broke it to us. But he liked it when Seng read the day's paper aloud to him. None of you others know how to space it properly, he said. Like he's just telling it to you.

Back in his room, he would ask me, several times an hour, to hold the glass of water for him while he took sips through a straw. Not long into the final day when the family sat about the bed and he drifted in and out of sleep, he said with a sudden firmness that had not been there for some time, 'If what I say comes out tangled you know what I mean to say. Right?'

It is not a thing I would say to another living being, and it does not say much to my credit, but I felt a disappointment I know I should be ashamed of. That Grant's last words were so banal. Like closing a meeting, more than a life. Yet how dare I think that?

Lou I think guessing that I thought so.

Lou was Grant's closest friend since their time together at school, then university. After that, in this country or that. It seems I had known him almost as long. He flew across from Brisbane when I phoned to say that this was probably as wise a time as any for him to come.

At home, and then again at the hospice, they liked the chance to sit, just the two of them together. Taking each other for granted, as they had for forty years. Good to see Lou there, waiting, reading, tapping at his iPad, when Grant stirred from his 'bursts of sleep'. That's not the way I should say it is it? Smiling. Grant's slight mistakes amusing him. I guessed that both of them, these two old friends, knew it was something of an act, these last days together. Lou spoke of it later and I was surprised at how astute it was. 'The charade,' as he said, 'when we are most serious together. We can't help theatre coming into it.' Their lifelong banter, like the kind when I drove Lou from the airport directly to Grant, who asked, without attempting to stretch out his hand, 'So how am I looking?'

'Ratshit,' Lou said.

'I was hoping you'd say that.' And then Lou leaning over him, his hand moving across Grant's forehead as though he were stroking a tired child, and his friend's hand was there too, holding Lou's wrist.

Lou who had altered so much less than Grant over the years. The same weight, given a few kilos, since they had played in the same rugby team, his tightly curled hair silvering, you wanted to say, rather than turning white. That same mix of directness and hesitancy as when he had served in his mother's shop, speaking in another language if they were alone together. Never married, brilliant at running his research company, still as left-wing as when he and Grant (imagine that now!) read Marx together the same summer as they picked fruit in Central as students. The kindly and distant family friend in Brisbane, generous when as teenagers the children went across to stay with him, insisting he was simply 'Lou', as he was with us.

I guessed some time back that he was less easy in a room if there were only the two of us. But as Delia has said to me time enough over the years, with her wry assessing directness, It's not as if you're the sharpest when it comes to judging people, Mum. That's the vanity, I suppose, of someone who went into theatre for a career. Have you ever noticed that? How actors, who can hollow themselves out completely, the better to leave room for characters to fit in, rather fancy themselves at reading other people? Thinking how they would play them, more likely. A very different thing from knowing what makes them tick. Grant inclined to tease me when he thinks I am putting the children, or anyone if it comes to that, 'under the lamp', as he calls it. Don't try to explain them, he says.

'Every love story, every death story, ends up being much the same.' I heard some visiting writer say that, or something very like it, at a festival event I once attended. It comes to mind sometimes as I devour one novel after another, and in a year's time am likely to have forgotten the details of the story that at the time held me as if I were being enlightened by them. Delia said much the same, although speaking more widely than just of novels, that so many were really the same story over again. She thought that was something in their favour. Unlike Jamie, who said matter-of-factly when he was about fifteen, that he thought English, apart from grammar and teaching us to say things correctly, was pretty much a waste of time. But now I'm onto Delia. She is the one who knew from age ten what she intended to be. 'I'll be her one day,' as she used to say when someone on television caught her fancy. Grant believed her before I did. 'Because it's not the glamour stuff she says that about,' he said. 'It's the older women, noticed that? Or some unattractive kid.' Certainly neither of us stood in her way.

When the children visited we often sat in what we grandly called 'the conservatory', which was simply a side veranda of the old villa glassed in on three sides, with rather colourful plants hanging down in baskets among the ferns. The room faced north, and on winter days when it could be frosty outside until lunchtime, it was a delight to sit in there to chatter on. In Grant's last months it was where we spent a great deal of our time. Even with the family there, we might often go for an hour without speaking, the children reading too, or scrolling on their phones, while their dad dozed. We knew of course that time was running down, which both of us feared; we knew what was inevitable, but for each other's sake we said, No, we will not let it rule the time we have. Grant, as I think of it now, must have known that there was something of a charade about this, glossing reality with talk that distorted fact. But no, Delia said later when she and I talked about it, that was where people so misunderstood how 'performance' carried a necessity of its own, a different truth from the kind most people are at ease with. Then of course, before the end of the year, there we were in the church we so infrequently attended, the two girls hand in hand as if again they were children, and Jamie, for all his business with the dying, was the one who found it hardest to speak, to find the words that came to the girls so much more readily.

Time the healer. The dawn after the dark. Nothing stands still. The well-meaning consolations we want to believe but think unlikely, and then one day realise they are clichés for a reason. Because what they say is the case.

Rachel is the one I have seen more of during the past two years, just down the road as she said, then recently to her apartment in Mt Eden. This boyfriend or another sometimes with her, always introduced as 'my new friend, Mum,' never as intimating more than that. Until one morning when I drove cartons of her books up for her, now that the house is on the market, far too large as I say for just one person rattling about in it. And to tell the truth I have let it go down rather. The conservatory overgrown until any charm it had was lost as it became unkempt. My losing interest in the house—in most things—for several months, but even after that, when life picked up, and I travelled across to Australia and could not get over how attractive it was, in a way I had never been open to before. I knew it would be no more than a matter of sorting things out, and I would be glad to move.

I texted Rachel to come down to help with carrying the books inside. It was ten o'clock, and she still wore a kind of Japanese housecoat that came to her knees. She was grinning as I pulled into the grass verge, near one of the trees that make the streets round where she lives so attractive. A man the same height as herself, with short blonde hair and a kind of shyness in the way he stood back a little, smiled at me and took me in with a quick, almost furtive, glance.

'This is Derek,' Rachel said, much as she had introduced me every year or so to young men with names like Rory or Sam or Muru. Only this time she said, 'We're getting married, aren't we, Derek?' and he said, 'Sure are,' in a way that made me feel far more than the decades between us. And then any trace of what I had first taken as reticence gone in a flash, as he opened the door for me and hugged me and said, 'We've this bottle on ice, we'd better do something about it,' and within minutes the three of us drinking from Briscoes flutes, and I was liking at once my daughter's fiancé's warmth.

'IT,' he said, 'that's why I'm working from home.' And I said, inanely, so wishing someone else was here to say things for me, 'It seems half the people your and Rachel's age do the same.'

Derek went down to the car and carried up the boxes. 'But some of these are from *school*!' Rachel said. 'Why on earth I ever kept them!'

'In case you kept failing,' Derek said, his hand running down the bamboo pattern of her cut-off gown. 'In case you had to sit your exams again.'

Later in the day I said, 'Fate couldn't have been kinder.'

Then when Derek went out, there were just us girls together and it was the easiest thing in the world to tell her. And I said, 'Well, that's the toughest part over.'

'Fingers crossed.'

I felt it was hardly something I could speak of with Delia except face to face. Why did that phrase 'the least I owe her' so jump to mind? She laughed when I told her so, in a Lebanese restaurant, the food as plain as the furniture, but she said it had to be near the Belvoir, you wouldn't believe how Chekhov of all people seemed to bring out the worst in people in rehearsals. The director's wife wasn't coming back, she meant it this time, and there were endlessly ruffled feathers about accents. 'No,' the director shouted to the lead, in front of the whole cast, 'Madame Ranevskaya did *not* come from fucking Redfern, darling.'

She had me in stitches. She knew well before I got to it what I had come this far to say. 'My God, Mum, we're like Chekhov people ourselves. Everything said except what is obvious. I've known for months how it was going to end.'

She looked at me, and she must have picked up my surprise, my obtuseness. She looked at her watch then, and tapped it as if with someone else's imperious finger. 'The theatre and the guillotine. Some smartarse said the two things you can't be late for and expect to get away with it.' She kissed my cheek. 'I'll phone you at Lou's. I've got his number.' She waved from the entrance. My thespian daughter with a life of her own.

Jamie and I were more straightforward together, I had always thought. We saw things in a far less complicated way than the girls, who as teenagers argued with anyone who was up to it about politics or religion or feminism, while Jamie was content to get on with his career, knowing from the time he was a third former what he wanted to do with his life. I remember his patiently saying to me about his sisters, 'All this carrying on. They have to do it, you know. Clear the decks.' And in case I was not following him, 'To make room for themselves. Girls have to do that more than we do.' I was a little in awe of him after that. Did he take in his parents with as sharp an eye?

Yet as an adolescent, he was the one I feared for. I hated watching him play rugby, but was delighted when he won a school tennis tournament in his last year. I remember too watching him hugging himself against the wind as he stood at the edge of the school pool, waiting for his race to begin, his paleness almost blue in the cold. Everything in the afternoon ran together in the blur of my tears. Something in my eye, I pretended, there's so much grit in a wind like this. And my now making a mistake so huge it startled me. For he was the one, I kept telling myself, who understands. We will not need words to spell it out. And yet Jamie now, in his comfortable apartment overlooking the lake near the hospital. Before I had finished telling him, finished *beginning* to tell him. His hands flung up, melodramatically, I would have thought, had it been one of the girls. Not yet in tears, but angry. Seng, I noticed, had quietly closed the door of the lounge where we sat. The vein in Jamie's neck thickened into a cord, as when he was upset as a child. I held my hands in my lap. In that way our minds play with distractions when we fear where disagreement may lead, I thought how he had told me the colour of the walls behind his black leather furniture was called 'Amber Ice', and how meaningless the words were.

'Well fuck you, Mum!' He broke a pencil he had taken up from a table, a gesture that would have seemed staged had I seen it in a movie. But now Jamie hating me. Not what I told him, he said, that kind of shit was everywhere. But *me*, for what I was doing to Dad.

I did nothing, I tried to tell him. This is not then, it's now.

As if you can fucking separate life out like that! No longer holding back his tears. A boy with his hands covering his face. Seng came back into the room, and stood behind him, his hands on Jamie's shoulders, his turned cheek lying against his hair. My mind cutting across the sadness of what was happening between us. Thinking too how children almost always love stories about how their parents met, what they first saw in each other. What it must have been like, at the beginning, before the likelihood of their existing. Not that they ever really tell us, our parents, but that has nothing to do with our wanting to know. I thought how among the few things that Jamie said he would like, when I first spoke of selling the house, was an enlarged photo that had lain in an envelope for years, in a desk drawer. It was Grant and me, six months before we were married. Neither of us took great photos, but this, by some chance of light, some catch of mood, was close to glamour. Grant's head tilted, but the shadow itself was handsome, his arms folded on his bare chest, his looking directly at me, and I was in a long muslin dress, the shape of my figure clear through the backlit cloth, our turning towards each other, unaware of anything but each other. A rare image of what love indeed might look like.

I knew as clearly as if it had been dictated to me, what I must say to Seng as he walked with me down to the car. 'He will want to kill that photo he took from the house last time you were over. Don't let him do that will you? Hide it somewhere so he won't be sorry later on?'

Seng touched my arm. 'I won't let him.'

When I spoke to my sister about marrying again, in those weeks when it seemed I seldom slept, worrying about how I would tell the children, imagining how each might take it when I told them, Mary, who is a year older than me to the day, said she remembered so little about him from 'back then'. She had to look at old school magazines and the few photographs she had of my wedding when Lou was best man. Outside an ornately official *mairie* in a small Riviera town. The two men wearing ties, the woman who was our other witness a friend of Lou's, who had sprained her ankle later in the evening, after our dinner in a palm-thatched restaurant that was meant to have a Pacific ambience, which meant the waitresses wore leis and Gauguin prints were on the walls. Then our not really catching up again for years, until the children were growing up.

Mary had this curious memory, though, of an evening at a university tournament when we had gone to see Grant boxing, and Lou was fighting too, in a lower division. I'd quite forgotten until she mentioned it. And then surprised me when she said what had stuck with her was not Grant's fight, but that Lou was so pale. Each time his body was hit, a blotch showed on his skin. He was deft and tough but by the end of three rounds he looked like the illustration in a medical textbook, his skin bloomed like an affliction. The memory amused her. And she said with that brisk certainty I was never quite at ease with, 'They're grown up for God's sake. Forget this 'children' racket.'

I say things to Jamie I know are sincere, but by the time

they reach across a room can sound hollow, even trite. 'He's kind, he's thoughtful, he makes me feel alive. Not nervy about myself.' I do not say, he wants me, yes, like that, which matters too. 'I'm not just ashes,' I try to tell Jamie. 'Just because I'm a widow.'

'No,' he says. 'But you're not two people either.' His friend Seng sometimes places his hand across Jamie's, but smiles at me, the light slipping across his jet-black hair as his head moves slightly, and we know, the three of us know, he is comforting me as well. Later he visits twice by himself to meet Lou, and I can tell they understand each other. 'Give it time,' as each of them tells me. Lou makes him laugh. They tell each other weakly amusing jokes. 'We're allowed to be racist together,' Seng says. Lou looks at him with affection. 'We've earned our stripes.'

Last evening I began to nod off while they talked quietly. After what seemed an age of worry about what was simple enough, I felt my eyes grow heavy as Lou's and Seng's voices twined together. Lou said, his brushing my knee with his knuckles, 'We'll still be here talking when you wake up. That right, Seng?' I leaned back on the big cushion. They were talking about the Far Field. From when Lou and Grant were at secondary school together.

There was a rugby paddock to the side of the shallow river terrace where the school's classrooms stood, and the big assembly hall. Beyond that, like an over-sized ditch, a gully with coiled blackberry and scraggy trees and and a surface that turned to mud after a day's rain. And further still, on the gully's other side, the Far Field, immaculate with its marked-out running track, its cricket pitch, and at its edges, the practice nets. I could never quite catch the reverence that tinged the way it was spoken of. On term sports days, on the big occasions when other schools competed, the girls from High and Sacred Heart would tease and speak of it for a week. But you *must* be going? Mustn't you? The Far Field?

I remember the bright avid groups ranged along the white-marked lines. The athletes desperate to shine. As Grant almost did, in the quick short races. While almost evasively, Lou, who was shorter than most yet a fine middle-distance runner, had no sooner won than he managed to be out of sight. And someone telling me, 'He has to get back to help in the shop. Saturday afternoons especially.' The Dally fish and chip shop, where his mother's huge bosom swung as she lifted the wire baskets from the boiling vats and turned to shake them onto the opened pages of old newspapers. Not that he was always back at the shop as he made out he had to be, I heard him now explaining to Seng. His fingers quietly opening and closing on my knee. Lou saying, and his new friend quietly laughing, 'I didn't always want to be hanging round.'

A lifetime simply to learn that, about the Far Field.

MARY'S BOY, JEAN-JACQUES

He sprang from the cabin window . . . upon the ice raft which lay close to the vessel. He was soon borne away by the waves, and lost in darkness and distance.

—The last lines of *Frankenstein*, Mary Shelley (1818)

I

It is as if the ice is pressing its grip on the very fact of existence, so even the line between its surface, and the sky above it, is taken on trust. It is the paralysing fang of life itself. It attempts to make us part of its vast domain. So Captain Sharpe thought of it, his mind stiff with insistence, groggy with cold and what he sipped to combat it.

His head leaned back on the handsome panelling of his cabin, its appearance as near to a replica of his hero's own immortal craft, but half a century further on. He was fifty-three, Captain Francis Sharpe, which placed his birth in the year when the American colonies grew restive. He was from a wealthy and secluded family. As such persons frequently do, he traced his own line of ancestry against the expanses of history with a curiously modest pride, defender of the old religion, born into comfort and the instability of a family which, for more than two centuries, had never found quite the venue that did justice to its gifts. With his extensive cabinet of maps and charts, he recorded day by day the movement of the *Dorothea*, its temporary position on the great hip of the globe. As again, in yet another dimension, parallel with the reality of our shared measurable world, there was the movement of his soul, that most profound of human facts.

Captain Sharpe drew his bearskin closer. Deposits of ice were packed even inside the cabin, against the squares of glass on the curved wall that allowed a dull greyish light to break into the stillness of where he sat. Another and younger man, his lieutenant and distant kinsman, huddled at the small board of his own desk, a simple plank that a brass chain allowed to be lowered from the panel above his chair. Neither man had spoken for some hours. Something of the ice's silence seemed to fall between not only the officers but the ship's lower orders as well, in their padded canvas wraps below decks, men as driven into their own thoughts or the spells of sleep they shuddered from, back to the latent madness of where they were.

A small coal fire, in its bolted iron stand, was like the eye of an animal in the heavy gloom. Or so young Jackson thought from time to time, as his own head nodded and then again was righted. He disliked the way his mind so effortlessly turned to fantasy, to such pointless images. For all one's science, one's freedom from the persistent haul of superstitions, these moments when the mind nosed loose like another animal itself. He looked across the narrow space of the master's cabin, held, as he so often was, by the distant relative who fascinated him.

The captain eased his fur cap against the wall behind him. The ear that a flap had covered now stung in the freezing air. His forefinger delved at an itch inside his collar. There was a sudden creaking of the ship's timbers, breaking the stillness of which the ship's progress seemed so solemn a part. There were times when he felt he must stand and move, to break the sense that he too was hardening into immobility. Earlier in the day—in the late morning, in fact, but exactness of time had so little to do with the meagre uniformity of light—he had forced himself to go on deck. He forced himself to stand in the frigid air for longer than seemed bearable, the scooped shell of the sky arcing above him. The ropes were iron hard. Ice daggered the spars. A floe, several times the size of the ship, lay placidly level with them, perhaps a mile off to starboard. Where one side rose and thinned, its whiteness shaded to an immaculate pale blue. Without turning, he knew that some of the crew were watching him. The master of his vessel is never unobserved. The men were here because that was the nature of their calling: to endure so their families, in distant shires, might survive. But at sea there is one master. His life determines theirs. Every skill at his disposal must be alert for their care. He prayed that he do it justice, the trust they placed in him.

As he prayed to understand himself. Unlike young Jackson, who frankly spoke of his unease in the latitudes they now traversed, the captain was unperturbed. Space and time were like great walls surrounding him, which he refused to take as absolute. They were there, real as his own flesh, yet speaking somehow for more beyond themselves. His body might be subject to them, but not his mind. The mystery enlivened rather than appalled him. His lieutenant's vague grasp at comprehending what the older man might think fed his own ironic certainty that, for all his fine seamanship and decency, his relative was not the sanest man to sail with. But then Jackson's own incentives, another man might also question.

At an hour when on land great cities hummed, there was the first cry from the watch, the first piercing perhaps ever of a human voice within a hundred miles. Then its echo without time enough to come back before the pelting of the iron bell, its pulsing out across the ice, the black channels of the sea. The crew's startled leap into activity, the rush and hollering as the men swore and emerged, hauling on their bulked-out pea jackets, their fleeced hoods and thickly knitted caps, as they thudded from the below decks. The release from seemingly endless boredom, the unexpected breaking to excitement rousing them to a raw pitch of shouting, the bell summoning them to the strangeness of the light. For this was near midnight, as the captain's chronometer could confirm, yet a needle might still be threaded by a steady hand.

The clamour of the bell began to fade, as did the shouting of the men. Captain Sharpe took up his customary place on the elevated deck. The heavy bear-fur thickened his bulk, squaring him to appear more squat than his five feet six inches. A silence fell across the ship. The strangeness of the men standing below him at this hour, in this stolid and distant world, in their ignorance of why they had been roused with such urgency, brought to the captain's own mind the momentary thought that all this was illusion. But the lieutenant's quiet interruption, 'Sir?', at once drew him back to where they were, to what he was about to impart to his crew. The young Swede who had been on watch and so hauled them to the alertness they now shared, stood beside the captain, speaking with him, moving his arms in excitement, seeking the English words from the limited store he had to draw on.

The captain spoke simply, with his usual directness. 'God has put a rare gift our way,' he said. For as always, he acknowledged that ours is to some extent a shadow world, and not a living soul's true home. Yet he was too fine a seaman, too practical in the purposes of his craft, to more than acknowledge as much, before turning to the moment. At first he raised the bronze extension of his spyglass, swinging it across the Swede, who rapidly stood back, and focused it for several minutes, on whatever it was he so attended to. The crew, and Lieutenant Jackson within an arm's length of his captain, held their breaths as if by consent.

The captain had removed his glove, the better to work the milled screw of the telescope with precision, as he swept the bright enlarging circle in its quest for what the Swede has sworn he had seen, perhaps less than a league away, on one of the almost imperceptibly drifting floes. He scanned in detail the low ridged crags, the pocks of scooped caverns, before the movement of the spyglass stopped, and held steady. Only the lieutenant caught the quick inhalation of the captain's breath, his declaring, 'Dear God!', a voice barely above a whisper. For in the detailed circle he commanded, in the white and black clarity of what he saw, and yet its pervading sense of leprous greyness, he saw the movement young Larsen had noted ten minutes earlier, before he reached for the frozen rope that had swung the bell to life.

The captain's hand slightly shook as his entire being coursed along his line of vision towards the black, humped, distorted creature, crouched as if in some kind of terminal combat with the ice. It came to him as a physical pain, when the reality jabbed at him. The realisation that what he watched could only be a fellow being. While at the instant that he thought so, the inexplicable contrary push of his mind, that no, this could not be so. For how lucidly it also came to him, that the ragged figure he looked at so gave the impression of burrowing, convulsing, as if its entire drive was not to be rescued, but to escape further away, as if *into* the ice itself.

He at once called his instructions, the crew moved quickly to carry them out, and Mr Jackson descended the companionway from the bridge to join the men. All fell into the efficiency of a crew at ease with its command, of officers respected by those beneath them, quickly shaping what had been a loose and indeterminate swirl into a capacity to obey. The captain called to lower a boat. There was a life to be saved. He did not remark, even to his lieutenant, that from here onboard, with the limitations of distance, and the uncertainty of the frosting glass, there was something in the long quiver of the bootless figure he observed, its upper body concealed by garments drawn against it, that already burdened him. There was something monstrous—yes, even that—in what he saw.

Evans, the taciturn Bible-obsessed first mate, as inflexible and reliable as a length of tempered steel, had manoeuvred the pinnace close against the flank of its ship. Four men sat ready with raised oars as Mr Jackson lowered himself by rope, rather than the ladder he might at other times have descended by, and took his place facing the men. The boat quickly angled away from the ship's side. For those watching from the rails of the *Dorothea*, it cut quickly through the seemingly polished black surface of the water, a frill of white showing along the beat of the blades.

It was a matter of ten minutes from the ship to the low shelf of ice, which tilted as Evans reached up with the long-poled hook that bit into its surface. The oars were shipped, the hook made fast with its trailing rope, the boat drawn in so the two forward men, each with grappling spikes in their hands and coiled rope looped on their shoulders, raised themselves to the level of the first shelf, and then higher on the slightly banking slope. They were no more than a dozen yards from whatever it was they had been charged with saving. And yet so close as this, the men were no more aware of what kind of man Fate, or God, or mere happenstance, had so drifted towards them, beyond an immediate apprehension as they watched the jerk of the exposed and naked legs, the now far more subdued movement of the huge upper body in its clutch of canvas strips, its scraps of fur. It was as though they watched a living being on the verge of expiring. Yet its upper body was attempting still to conceal itself from those who, surely by now, it understood came to him with only goodwill?

It was challenging work to turn the bulk of the creature, who was not unconscious but chose to do little of his own will to assist the men who passed a rope twice about his body, before hitching it beneath his armpits, then the end of the rope flung back to those in the boat, for Evans and the other oarsman to haul on, as well as the men still kneeling on the floating ice. The mass of ragged clothing that he wore bunched further with its dragging, while a folded canvas was passed up from the boat, and the body rolled onto it, and smaller ropes ran from the brass eyes at the corners to the main hank the men hauled at. The careful positioning movement, the shouting voices, the drag of the body across the bumping and slide of the freezing surface beneath it, brought the rescued bulk to where it angled forward, using its own strength to balance and step down into the boat. Mr Jackson, from his position at the pinnace's bow, saw for a moment the head level with his own, before the figure sat, and the small craft tilted wildly with the sudden weight and force of what now entered it. For there was now no likelihood of his rescuers thinking that what they rowed back towards the *Dorothea* was a man as they defined themselves. Another dimension had come among them. No one spoke as the oars plashed and the pinnace headed back to the ship where the crew now stood at the rails and the captain held the glass constantly against his eye.

Whatever they had rescued raised his eyes to take in those who had found him. There was dullness in his glance, but nothing of animosity. The rowing men raised their heads briefly to look at him, then quickly lowered their gaze. But their covert glancing enough to register how he sat far more than a head above the tallest of them, and the inordinate length from below his swollen eyelids to the slanted thrusting of his jaw. Beneath the scraps of tow-like hair and the patched paleness between its tufting, the disfigured brow whose swollen ridge was as if some crude incision has been dragged across it, and the skull closed like an ill-fitting lid. Evans the first mate shielded his sight from so aberrant a creation. In his certain belief in the persistent battle between good and evil, the monstrous might serve only one master. Where others in the crew felt simply human awe, or fear, or in time the possibilities of pity, Evans saw incarnate darkness. He would bide his time.

The figure would lie for days in a cubby the carpenter had knocked together. The cubby was set below the captain's favoured spot to stand on his own deck, from which the crew might be in sight beneath him, or observed as they worked the sails, or clambered the rigging. Their 'spidering', as it amused him to remember, his wife's droll description when she paid a rare visit aboard the ship that bore her name, and her family fortune paid for.

Only Captain Sharpe, and young Jackson, saw anything of him in those first days. A chain was put across the deck, past which the crew were not to pass, with the exception of the carpenter, who had some elementary grasp of physic. Enough at least to read something into a man's condition by his water and his stool, and who had rough but practical knowledge for dealing with men's ailments, from wens, to fractured limbs, to aching teeth. As a naval man in his younger years he had more than once been called upon to confirm that a man was dead after execution. Beyond this knack for bodily repair, the carpenter was a man without curiosity, perhaps the one man onboard who might be relied upon not to quiz in any way the creature he nursed, and brought grub to, and disposed of his waste. That was simply what he did, as part of his reason for being onboard. But because the captain, who spoke with him frequently, referred to his charge always as 'the guest', that was the word the carpenter repeated when referring to him among the crew, and so what generally he was called.

The captain accepted some of what was reported to him of his guest, and silently rejected other details, or held his opinion as moot. The guest does not, the carpenter assured him, feel natural conditions as we might, sir. His surviving the ice bore witness enough to that. Now he offered the example of an oil lamp accidentally dropped on an extended foot. The oil spilled when the glass had shattered and the flame continued to flare. 'On his naked leg, sir.' When the captain failed to answer, he insisted, 'Not like us, captain, that's all I'm saying.' The guest lay silent mostly, but sometimes spoke softly, but not so he could be understood. As if not in the way God intends most of us to speak.

'Not English?' the captain asked.

'Grunts and growlins,' the carpenter said. 'Perhaps like Scotch would say things.'

'Prayers?' Captain Sharpe asked.

No, not that he could say so, the carpenter said. 'I would know the sound of a prayer.'

But little else he might report. The guest lying for long hours, with his eyes closed, but not asleep.

'No sign of distressing dreams, of guilt, or fear?' The captain putting these questions to him as well, but reading incomprehension in the fellow's face.

'He's not one for knowing much about, captain.'

'Thank you,' the captain said. 'I'm grateful for anything

you might think I should know.' He knew his men valued his kindness, his courtesy.

In three days' time, as he came up to the bracing air after the cabin's night odours, Captain Sharpe saw the towering form dressed decently against the cold, its tufted hair weed-like above the slabs of its cheeks. There was a moment as each looked towards the other. The captain, with a curious politeness that went unobserved by any of his crew, touched the edge of his cap with a certain formality, which had no suggestion about it of mockery. The face that looked towards him on the higher deck was vivid and grotesque in the light's clarity. It was as if each attempted to read past the features that confronted him, to what kind of mind it was that he must deal with. For each understood that the rescue from the ice had drawn one to the other in some kind of compact. The future of each now depended on the other. For the moment, no other fact took precedence to that.

God knows, Captain Sharpe considered, what there might be about the guest that there was yet to learn. He could well understand why his crew, apart from young Jackson, so feared the form he now looked down on, with its intimidating bulk, the distortion of its features, as though what one face as it were attempted, another version marred. What most held the ship's master was the swollen ridge, like a length of barely fleshed hemp, running the breadth of the forehead to the gristle above the temple on the other side. For all its ugliness, the impression of an intelligence of some kind, a *disposition* being the word the captain chose. And whatever one assigned to it, his certainty that this too was a creature of the same divinity that shaped himself. Briefly, his mind held the absurd notion of the guest fleeing, concealed in the thickets of Eden, in the Garden's unpeopled places, eluding the edicts imposed on our own forebears. Yet, no, whatever else, he was one of us. *My brother, for all that.*

And this, the most startling link occurring between them. The guest tilted his head, so it was possible to see into the eyes that met his own, as the captain chose to believe, with a certain sympathy, even as they repelled. The yellowish lids were without lashes; there was no discernible ring separating the iris from the rest of each eye's sphere. Later, he would realise that a trick of slanted light had played its part in this impression. He would look again at his guest's eyes and note a clearer definition, the brilliant black pupils like the heads of nails in the discoloured murk surrounding them. The captain wondered at this, and much else. Did this almost man look at us, finding in us distortions of what he hoped for and understood, as we did in perceiving him?

But that first meeting on the deck. The scrutiny each brought to the other. The sense, sudden as a flare in front of them, of a concussion—even that—throwing them together. For when at last he spoke, Captain Sharpe said simply, but not expecting to be understood, 'You are a welcome guest.'

The stranger answered, as if this were no more than a polite exchange.

'Thank you,' he said. And then, *'Bonjour.'*

But the question of Captain Sharpe.

Why was the *Dorothea*—under the command of a man in his later middle years, honourably retired from the service, good-natured and indifferent to what most men would regard as conventional ambition—sailing in such remote and dangerous waters, in the Arctic summer?

For the next two hundred years, philosophers will refine

the question, and the possible answers: how does one cope with the *angst*, which increasingly is accepted as being at the core of our being human? For Captain Francis Sharpe, it may seem that naive envy in turn provoked a spiritual distress, which drove him to hazard a family fortune into the small matter of his ambition to match his hero, Captain James Cook, RN. What did the greatest Yorkshireman leave for maritime ambition, on anything but a minor scale, to be fulfilled? Is everything from his death, beneath the cudgels of his charted Pacific, to be a mere footnote to one of his masterful pages?

Yet the impulse survives, even if *pointlessness* becomes the constant and necessary word. If anything of ambition falls in the towering shadow of Cook, then surely a certain point *of some kind* might still be salvaged? Not a glorious and admirable and enduring point, but not one without a certain dignity, a kind of polished folly? In a word, the triumph of a disappointed man? The captain explained the notion first to his wife, who said good-humouredly that he must not expect her enthusiasm to equal his for this game with boats, as if the expanse of the oceans were not much more than a village millpond. And her adding, it was not as though he were still a young man.

'Time is not of the essence,' he answered her. 'There is no question of exploration or discovery.' He was modest as he explained it to her. 'I intend no more than to link one Pole with the other. Its scientific purpose is nil. It is for no other reason than I choose to do it. And no one else has done so. I do it merely to show it might be done, for no other reason but itself.'

He explained more fully to his kinsman Jackson when first they met, how there would be no call for marines, for armed men, for a bevy of clever scientific men to journey with them.

'A sturdy crew of honest and experienced seamen. I calculate we might do it with a few dozen men. Englishmen, for the greater part. Those whose temperament we understand. Where possible, with mates who have served under the colours, and two gentlemen as senior officers.'

'You seem to have great faith that it might actually be done?'

'As good a phrase as any,' Captain Sharpe said. He knew young Jackson might baulk a little at the words.

As he also knew that what he had in mind would mean little to the maritime world, beyond an occasional grudging nod over a rummer when his name was raised. For the wider world again, among the ignorant, the indifferent, among the increasingly bitter cry of those who would challenge any notion of class or gentlemanly ambition, it will be a crumb, dropped over a ship's rail into the moiling seas of time. Why should such a thing as he intends, be done at all? No reason, but the challenge itself. A way at least to declare that *here* was the kind of man who, with the fortune of earlier times, may have been called to do finer deeds than fate later allotted him. Oh yes, Francis conceded, the future indeed is shrouded as it is for any enterprise. But as he repeatedly assured his wife, now, in their lived moment, what the unknown may hold is a poor argument to raise against a man of honour.

The *Dorothea* was not an identical replica of any of his hero's celebrated vessels. It was built to a more modest scale, yet was similar enough for an expert eye to note the homage of resemblance. Over the twelve months of preparation, the sheer wilfulness of his intended and erratic course seemed not so much to recede from Francis Sharpe's mind as to take on a compelling logic. In the last few months before departure, he drew warmth from young Jackson's increasing excitement.

A boy, as his elder kinsman thought of him, caught up in the rancid enthusiasms of the time, stoked full of liberal notions, a reader even of Voltaire. But as cousin Richard amusingly told him, he had friends who were more disturbed by his having Romanist relatives than if he had confessed to owning slaves. That each so thought the other unconventional assisted the bond between them. And although the captain was not aware of it until they sailed, the lieutenant kept close to him his own passion for the protracted journey south, which once hearing of, his cousin approved of mightily. Sharpe felt a balance of a kind between their differing reasons for so desperately wishing for a journey that offered so little, apart from the singular fantasy of what promoted it. Yet how much altered course, after the Northern Pole, as the lieutenant wrote, 'magnetised us to such different forces'.

Lieutenant Jackson made regular notes in what the captain took to be his journal, that common enough form of writing between rumination and fact, which educated men of his generation were apt to keep while at sea. Their first response to what up to then they may no more than have guessed at, and yet an attempt as well to rope their journeying back to what they valued, to what they knew. A journal might even be called the space where one man was written into another, the old world meshed with the hard realities of the new. What the captain credited the lieutenant with was not quite the case. His neat script was engaged more with random observations, notes without sequence, sudden shafts of perception. As other men have found to be the case, a confident, well-ordered, conventional mind finds it no easy thing to make its notes seem more than commonplace. That evening he had written:

'Nature will tolerate any deviations or excess, so long as the impulse is towards something *new*. Its imperative is always towards that.'

The captain was shrewd at reading his relative's temperament—impulsive, a little vain, riddled with current ideas, certain in his uncertainties. Much later, on one of the long smooth evenings off islands near the tropics, he would actually say, 'This is preliminary to nothing of consequence, Richard, but it occurs to me at times that the reality of sin, which you so dismiss, may cause a man no more stress than your grappling away with notions of total liberty, of nature in itself the explanation of all things. Your obsession in your way as my own with another. Your Rousseau, my Aquinas. But the two of us bobbing away much as the ship we travel in now, should the weather turn inclement.'

The younger man was amused at the way the captain put things, his thinking as though from another age. He filled his own glass again with Madeira, aware of the admirable but surely partly crazed man observing him, as they sat close enough that if either stretched out an arm, they would have touched. Yet inexplicable, he thought, that the captain's acceptance of the high stakes one played for, should you share his notion of God, caused him so little discomfort. Such complacency even, while he himself, unencumbered with such weights of superstition, with his clearer mind, at times felt anguished.

It was now several months since what both men habitually thought of as the rescue from the ice. While they spoke, or as the only sound in the cabin being the scratching of Jackson's quill or the captain's rustling with his charts, their guest sat quietly, unless directly addressed. His head, so much higher than those of the men seated in the same dark cabin, leaned against the oak panelling behind him. He liked the feeling of the board's thrumming behind him, the always forward driving of the ship. The big lamp hanging from above them, the wash of the sea against the bows. It did not bother the guest that no word came to him, that no word was necessary, to describe the sense of contentment that came on him. It was some time back since the captain, speaking to him as he usually did from the added height of the bridge, had said, 'You still have never offered us a name?'

'I have no name,' he had said. Then after a long pause, during which the captain looked at him intently, he said, as if this were all that might be known of him, 'I am. That has been enough.'

Mr Jackson, who stood beside the captain, smiled and said, 'Our untampered natural man.' There was an edge of irony, as he then suggested, but with conviction, 'We might call our man Jean-Jacques.'

It was a name, the captain agreed, that suited their guest far more than any English one might do. He would have felt uneasy with that, for the guest's guttural speech carried something so apparently foreign. But now that he was named, there seemed less awkwardness between them. They spoke more often. The officers were struck by what they termed his native wit. And by his ignorance of so much. As reasonable men, they agreed there was a debt, surely, to instruct him? They baulked at going so far as to call it 'civilise', although that was what at heart each meant.

Once they entered broader latitudes, and weeks of routine sailing, he had been invited to join them in the master's cabin. Its dimensions seemed to contract as he stooped to enter, and take his place on a rough-hewn chair the carpenter was called on to make for him. For the most part, on those first

156

evenings, he was silent, but listened with great attention. So much between the two men, with their considerate manner of speaking to each other, that eluded him. On later evenings the drift of their conversation came home more clearly to him. The captain, whose command of his ship was so absolute, sometimes spoke as though there were another command higher than his own, a belief which the lieutenant seemed not to share with him. There were things the captain said that were taken from a special book, and the words 'our maker' which explained what all things were. 'The Word,' he would say, that made us as we are.

Other things, which were less clouded to think of, he also noted. The gradations of what he realised was meant by 'rank', the great store set on the notion of 'obedience', and most of all, the sense that was always with him, of being apart. It was here that it first occurred to him, that there was a way of saying things which was not in fact the way at all. When you might think one thing, and say something else, so you understood it better. When you said the word 'like', and a flare was lit, and you could see so much further because of it. He noticed how often the two men whose company he was asked to share spoke in that way. Their conversation came to a point that slowed what they were saying, and they used that strange word, 'like', as if speaking of something else, then they continued because a problem had been solved.

So much about their talk enlightened him. He knew from the behaviour of most of the crew that his appearance continued to frighten them, as it had other people so long ago, in other places, before his time on the ice. But the captain and Mr Jackson, who must have wondered too as they looked at him, took care to address him, to attend to what he might answer them, with the kindness they showed towards each other. He came to understand that each considered him in a different way. He knew how observed he was, as the captain sat there behind his desk, between the pictures on the wall behind him, one of a man not unlike himself, in similar clothes, the 'great sailor' as he was called, the other of a young woman with a blue veil across her head, her hands spread above a book, whose name was Mary. He knew the captain spoke to Mr Jackson of his 'soul', and of 'the Fall', and the younger man, in turn, chose other words as the ones he favoured. 'Liberty' was one of them; 'natural man' was another. The guest knew how so often the discussion came back to himself. As more evenings passed when they sat together, they spoke more directly to him. Yet the increasing puzzle for him was how different everything now seemed. From then. From before. The images that disturbed him as they came to mind. The fear that had driven almost every step he took. The sometimes loveliness and then the hatred of what he had seen, but mostly hate.

'Companion', was the word he waited for, and took pleasure in. As he entered the cabin some evenings the captain would say, 'Ah, our companion,' and slant his opened hand towards the heavy chair. The lieutenant too smiled towards him. Conversation took up again between the officers. Soon enough, between the three.

So much they spoke of tutored him. The captain explained the charts to him, and how to read them. He explained the astrolabe, and on a run of clear and exquisite evenings, stood beside him on deck, pointing to constellations, to guiding stars. Back in the cabin, he related what they had observed to the metal sphere that stood beside his desk. The captain was amazed at how quickly the guest retained what he was told. But apart from simply saying 'God', as the two figures of such disparate height stood side by side beneath the intimidating rack of stars, the packed grains of the Milky Way, and remarking, 'Mother Mary,' as he noticed Jean-Jacques' eyes drawn back to the small painting, he did not attempt to instruct him in the certainties he held. For there had been a rough agreement between the captain and Mr Jackson that neither would press their views on their natural man during the long journey that lay ahead. Not that the crew, apart from those who had closer dealings with him, would lose their deep suspicion of him, their own referring to him as the giant, the freak, the monster. Mr Jackson said lightly to him as they stood near the taffrail, 'There is only the curve of the entire world for us to sail, Jean-Jacques, so we can freeze all over again.' He set out for him the distance they must travel, before their turning yet again, and climbing from south to north, then home to England. He guessed at the time the intended course might take, and asked, 'What do you make of that?'

There was a long delay before Jean-Jacques spoke, as though the question demanded a different kind of answer to what the lieutenant may have waited on. 'I think only of one day at a time. As if my thinking on more could matter in the least.'

Mr Jackson was moved at the vaults of loneliness that seemed to lie behind his companion's answer. It was unusual for him to speak so fully on what he felt. Yet as the captain had remarked of him, their guest showed less reticence the further they were from anything that touched him. It was only then, sitting for example with the ship's charts spread in front of him, taking in the reasoning for longitude and latitude, the orbits of the moon and the handling of a theodolite, that his raw intelligence came through.

'He has a fine mind,' Captain Sharpe said of him. 'So long as his intellect is unobstructed by *us*, by what he makes of our fellow men.'

Mr Jackson said, 'He never speaks of what he feels. All that remains an unopened book.'

They found it impossible to draw from him *anything* before the fact of the rescue. If asked, he would look at them with his incisive gaze, from which nothing could be read. The two Englishmen, intelligent and tolerant, accepted they must be content with what they knew this minute, however his quickness startled them. To know more of the expiring being they had come upon by fate, and saved as any humane persons would have acted, foundered as if at some intractable cliff.

Each of the men who sat with him most evenings wrote their observations, their intuitions, in their journals. The captain writing rather more than Mr Jackson, who already considered, without needing to speak of it any more than commit it to paper, the usefulness Jean-Jacques might yet come to play in his own remote but passionate project.

Before their guest tapped at the heavy door for those hours when he joined them, Captain Sharpe entered in the ship's official log the past twenty-four hours' maritime facts: the distance travelled since his previous entry, the disposition of winds and currents, the local hour from the timepiece fixed to his desk, the chronometric cross-checking with time as it stood at Greenwich. This last, once it was spelled out to him, holding Jean-Jacques' attention to the point that he smiled, if one might call it that, the thick line of his upper lip curving at one side. The exactness of what he had heard delighting him.

As Lieutenant Jackson once joked, so long as one arrives at its desired end, all sea voyages are the same, except where they are different. Their guest was struck by how regularly, how smoothly, the many affairs of the ship were attended to. Because each man onboard had been chosen by Captain Sharpe, his past voyages and occupations carefully considered, there was a sense of closeness between the crew and the man who commanded them. Francis Sharpe had gone so far—a thing unknown to most who worked at sea—as to speak with each about their families, their backgrounds, what they desired from life and what they feared. Within days of sailing from England, he was accepted as a man for discipline, on the instance of the one crew member who had brought strong drink onboard, concealed in his belongings. The captain stood by as the mate emptied the two bottles overboard. He assigned the guilty man to the ship's most menial duties for the following month, and reduced rations. But once the penalty was played out, the captain again treated him as he did any other, his grog allowance restored. The crew would do anything for a man who could punish moderately, and then forget.

Jean-Jacques would stand for hours beside his cubby below the captain's deck. He watched, as though endlessly fascinated, the men and their business of using the sea, working with it, accepting its mastery beyond what they had in mind. He did not feel closeness with the men, for apart from the carpenter and the boy assigned to bring him meals, it was a rare thing for him to speak with any of them. Yet he knew their names, and their characters. He observed them with more care than any would suspect.

Everything diverted him, although little surprised. He had no expectation, nothing to compare them against, except themselves. The most difficult thing to comprehend was how all onboard accepted as so natural what he saw as the unchallenged scale in the spaces between one man and the next. Not only between those who fitted the places assigned to them onboard, the inflexible distance between the captain and the senior crew, between them in turn and those beneath them, but a stranger matter again. How one man was different from another, quite apart from what the *Dorothea* expected of them. Why a smaller, quiet man was treated with respect by his fellow crew, and a large, talkative man was kept at length? Even of the same event, he noted how there could be such clarity and yet such concealment as well. So this was what *mankind* was like, beyond what he had known of it, before the ice? These were thoughts, as if at first straight lines, which broadened, which confused, the more he entertained them.

And so neither the captain, nor his lieutenant, might guess that by the time the *Dorothea* approached the fullest circle of latitude, and the men were permitted extra grog, and their stomping and singing continued into the night with its great audience of stars, Jean-Jacques felt a warmth that he guessed was what language meant by *affection*. He wondered, as he watched his hosts, and grew easy at being in their company in the evenings when they now sat together on the upper deck, rather than in the confining cabin, that what he knew would be called their *formality*, had changed as if with the mild weather as they ran in what the captain called fortunate seas. He thought of the great ice sheets, the broken fragments, some huge as hills, that had diminished until a time like now, the days when the sea was itself alone, a great circular expanse, and the ship at its centre. So hard to think of any world but this, the one they were in this minute, the mildness of the air that day by day stroked a swaying contentment into the fabric of the ship itself.

He heard the carpenter say for his own hearing alone, how 'blessed peace favours us'. The phrase puzzling him. It returned as he sat with Captain Sharpe and Mr Jackson, who were happy to accept long spells of silence, before a remark that might be no more important than the older man's saying how it surprised him that robins which had nested in a tree for years, then missed a year, again returned. He did not expect an answer. Any more than did Mr Jackson, when he laughed and remembered a time in some French port, under a famous and feared admiral, when a midshipman had failed to return before sailing, and was rowed out just in time to clamber a rope let down to him. The boy shaking with fear of the punishment he expected. And the famous admiral, who for some reason was less stern than usual, quizzed the boy, demanding had he been drinking, as crew on short shore leave were forbidden to do. No, the boy whimpered, not so much as a drop, had he not promised his mother? It came out that the midshipman had been snared by a woman in a private house, who had lied to him about the time. The small clock she had showed was deliberately set wrong. It was a matter, Mr Jackson said, of the crew waiting to hear how many lashes. But the admiral looked at the boy and even touched his handsome curls. He said a man returning drunk is a threat to the fleet, and by God, sir, that was something the middy should thank his mother for. But if within the week, there was the least discomfort of pox, he would know threefold what a whipped drunkard would feel for his vice. Mr Jackson remembered the men cheering as if with gratitude on the boy's behalf. He had never seen or even heard of anything to touch it in his years at sea. The captain laughed and said, 'That's Lewis for you, God rest him.'

Then there was silence again. The night calm enough one might scarcely hear a rope strain, or the timber creak. When the first mate came up and spoke to him, the captain said yes, the men might cast lines; an hour later, the odours of frying fish rising from the galley. Then sadly, perhaps, the captain said, clearly having thought more on Mr Jackson's story, 'I had neither Lewis's craftiness nor his sense of humour, to hold devotion the way he did.' Then another pause, before declaring, 'My own career was scarcely a distinguished one.'

'You are too severe on yourself, Francis,' Mr Jackson said. 'It was nothing, was it, to be in the fleet under Howe, for the Glorious First of June? Have the satisfaction of a French frigate raising the white flag to you? To be commended by the Admiralty?'

'It was scarcely Trafalgar,' Francis said. He passed over the detail of a recent wound that had forced him to shore for several months, at that very time.

'Cape Finisterre was a skirmish, you will tell me next?'

With a rare dab at humour, Francis said, 'Any engagement, irrespective of size, that Britain fails to win, is of course a skirmish.'

He was grateful to young Richard for his kindness. 'No, it was not quite nothing. But this matters more'—his meaning the journey they now shared. 'So much more.' He smiled across at the neat younger man in his trim uniform. Appearances matter so much to him, he thought. What distance there was between the two of them! There were moments, and this was one of them, when the captain admitted how others might find it difficult not to see vanity, as much as folly, in what he was about. But such moats of honesty were quickly enough leaped across. If a man believes his life fulfilled by what another dismisses as misguided, how might that alter his resolve by a jot? Against any argument that might be mounted, *I shall have done it.*

By the time the weather turned again, and the seas ran more turbulent, and gales heeled the ship so there was great urgency in how the sails were reefed, and the masts slid across the skies and held their lean for hours at a time, life on the *Dorothea* had changed. After the leisurely drift of time in the weeks before, there were days when massed clouds stacked above the horizon, breaking into lightning, bringing savage winds. The need for vigilance ran to weeks before the worst of the weather passed and the evenings in the captain's cabin were resumed.

Jean-Jacques noted freshly how the captain and Mr Jackson enjoyed each other's company, and yet how one might argue strongly, even raising his voice as if on the brink of anger, against the other. But when that happened, they soon enough laughed, or returned to speaking as they usually did. His own thoughts went back, beyond his willing them, to when he had watched a family through a wall, in the early times of what he would so dearly have forgot. An old man, the younger man and woman, the child. To how that time had ended, the red haze that came across his eyes when deep anger rose in him, as if that, so much more than anything else, was the deepest part of what he came to think of as *himself*. Not his mind alone, nor the body that he walked in. A point he could think beyond no further, once it was reached: I, who am separate from all other things.

Yet that other word he came to understand more clearly, the warmth as he thought on it. Companionable. The silence as the two men read, and himself a part of how all three sat cabined in such ease. The word the captain had used for it. *Our companionable soirée.* The captain would read silently, or at times aloud, as he offered details of what they might expect to glimpse tomorrow, among the now frequent islands the ship threaded between, some so close one might see the smoke rising from what would be a village or a town.

'Why does the ship not come more close to where they are?'

The captain told him then of piracy, which was common enough in these latitudes. There was no assurance that men who spoke another language would welcome men so different from themselves. He told him stories of the great seaman whose journals he read almost daily, whose engraving balanced the painting of the beautiful blue-veiled woman on the other side of the captain's desk, her hands spread a few inches above the book opened in front of her. It came to Jean-Jacques quite how much these friends already had taught him, how his mind was indeed like a living thing that needed such instruction to survive. Such distance as there now was between what he had been, and his sitting here *like a gentleman*, in the jacket a sail-maker had run up for him from three other garments made to fit ordinary men, a pair of trousers made to the same proportions, that covered him to his calves, and the boots that he wore only on these evenings, that reasonably enough were joked at, as if each foot were sunken into some eviscerated animal, such lengths of leather had been cut in shaping them.

Only two months had passed. So small a time, which he could credit no more than Lieutenant Jackson, who was amazed still at his extraordinary good fortune in coming closer than any other man he knew of to the wild forbear in whom the great Rousseau celebrated natural virtue. While his older cousin, with his mind so yoked to earlier times, knew that the giant surely must be, in some way he was unable quite to comprehend, explicable in terms of his own faith—a remnant of some strayed biblical tribe, a soul as dear to its Creator as he hoped his own to be. But while the captain was content to leave matters there, the lieutenant was the one more bothered not by what he knew of the creature he had named, but by what he did not. As he wrote in his journal, 'But what of *before*? As well expect enlightenment from the dead.'

And yet for the three of them, the remarkable moment that took their companionship to another place, hysterical, bacchic, and for gentlemen of an English cast, doused too in shame. Several further weeks had run their course. A tracing finger on the sloped globe would now seem midway between the equator's girth and the globe's dwindled southern pole. Storms and calms and temperatures rose and fell. The soirées had moved back into the master's cabin, a more confined atmosphere than when they had sat on deck and there was the marvellous sense at times of the craft being drawn on by the elements, as much as propelled by them. An evening when as usual the naval men drank liquor that held at its centre the reflected pip of light from the cabin's lantern, and Jean-Jacques clasped in his hand the lemon cordial the captain had poured for him. The sea had been, as he said, benign throughout the day. The cabin's desks were level as if set on solid land. When a huge swell suddenly took the ship side on, tilting it steeply so the panelling behind Captain Sharpe heeled back, his head thrown against it as though he sat on a sloping board. The decanter of burgundy slid across the desk. The captain lurched to grasp at it, with the consequence of his sleeve sweeping his glass to clatter against the fixed timepiece then balance against a rolled chart. From where he sat a few feet away, Mr Jackson leaped forward, his hand clipping the neck of the decanter, sending it into a spin, a stream of liquor spurting across his jacket. As the captain attempted to stand, his balance faltered so that he sprawled instead across the desk. A marble paperweight thudded to the boards and rolled with the tilt of the ship. For a fragment of time, the decanter too angled towards the floor, a slanting flash, as Jean-Jacques seemingly flowed in one dark fluid motion, like the movement of a shadow, his huge hand spread. The two Englishmen tumbled against him. The captain and his lieutenant were momentarily like schoolboys in some game of tugging against other. With one hand the stooping Jean-Jacques steadied the lieutenant, jerking him to his feet, and with the other raised the captain—all this in one swift, perfectly timed thrust across the cabin from his chair. He returned at once to where he had sat, and again crossed his legs, while the men he had untangled leaned, still with the ship's now altered motion, as it descended the other side of the wave. He nodded towards the half-filled decanter where he had placed it in front of the captain's chair, balanced by the red cushion the captain's wife had made for him. He now said, 'The wine is still there for you, captain.'

The sea's unexpected lift, the unbalancing of the decanter and the flying glass, the falling of the men like tangling boys, and then this, the parody as Jean-Jacques' words so seemed of *sang-froid* and poise, set even the captain into a high nervous kind of laughter, the usual world of order restored, but the absurdity of what occurred seething in them as well. The lieutenant, now that the tension had snapped, leaned with both hands on the arm of his chair, hooting, for that seemed the only word, his body heaving with a paroxysm that possessed him.

Nothing in Jean-Jacques' experience had taken him to anything like what he now watched and heard. The men he believed he knew a little more of each day were now in a place so far removed they were strangers to him. The captain's face reddened with the blurting sounds that came from him, through him, as an extended fart broke from him with the sound of ripping canvas. And in another lesser lurch of the ship, the lieutenant staggered towards Jean-Jacques, now placing his hand on his great shoulder for balance. The pressure of the man's hand worked strangely on him, as did the closeness of his bent head, the almost choking noise coming from his throat. For Jean-Jacques felt a convulsive catch in his own chest, his body forcing him towards something as yet unknown to him, a delight he could not suppress from racketing through him without his consent. A sensation that now owned him.

For all the agitation of his frame, the play and jerking of muscle and sinew that was so new to him, a touch of wonder as well. This rushing to him as he understood that the sound striking the cabin walls and rebounding from them, of course, was *laughter.* It sometimes came from the crewmen as they worked together, or *sported* as Captain Sharpe named it, in the free hours with their games with coiled circles of rope, or tossed blocks of wood. His comprehending that it was not a thing you owned yourself, but must come to with other people. A sound that said there is no *apart*, as everything else in his memory had so insisted. When the same thing is the same for them as well.

Then the rapid experience was over. The captain raised his recovered glass to him, and said we have you to thank, Jean-Jacques, for our wine and our lives. He understood that this must be a *joke.* The more the ship's guest comprehended words, the more it was clear to him how the very same word might keep its meaning, but the way it was said could so change how you must hear it. He noted something else as well. The Englishmen had liked it, had delighted in it, when his own laughter joined theirs. Yet there was an aspect to his laughter, its uncontrolled bellow, the deep raucous intake of breath when he felt his vision begin to blur, a sound which he knew discomforted them as well, for it was then that their own laughter ceased.

He soon after left the cabin. As always, he moved delicately for all his bulk. His chest continued to convulse. He stood at the ship's railing, close to the hut where he slept. That first unexpected swell which had thrown the men against each other, that brought on the confusion and hysteria and the fall of the decanter and his own instant dive to prevent its breaking, had been followed almost at once by a more rhythmic rise and falling of the sea, that continued through the night. He stood at the rail, which touched the chest of most of the crew but in his case failed to reach his waist. His lips tasted the salt from the spray flung up at him. A breeze was rising to stronger gusts. He held a strand of the rigging that reached into the darkness. There was no moon, no stars. The strange and exhilarating mood of the cabin had now quite gone. A drear heaviness came down on him. His loneliness at the centre of whatever world this was, the confusion of all that was new, in the weeks that followed his first moments as he had sprawled on the deck, with the men ordered to stand back from him, and the captain above him, his firearm sloped towards him, before the first words he had spoken, to prove that yes, for all his distortion, *Je suis un homme.* And yet the contradiction to that, a counter-current in his mind, the long other time, the other life, swirling in his mind. The years before the ice. The time of hunting and being hunted down, *before I was a man.* Before Mr Jackson, joking with him one evening, after the captain had called his praises for so quickly grasping the meaning of planetary motion, had teased and complimented him. 'So, you are joining the enlightened, Jean-Jacques.' The captain then adding, his meaning quite beyond their guest, 'The instructed, I would say, Richard, rather than the enlightened.'

That distance still between them. He watched a curling fringe of phosphorescence glimmer and slip away, and others follow it. He might understand even that, from what the lieutenant had explained to him. Sufficient at least for a natural fact not to seem a mystery. Mr Jackson had said, as they looked up to the stars from the slightly rocking deck, 'There are fewer mysteries by far, than there were not so long in the past, Jean-Jacques. By the time we return to England, imagine how much more than you are aware of even now, you will own as well.'

For the first time the officer placed his hand on the coarse fabric of his companion's sleeve. This done not in passing, but his hand left there long enough for Jean-Jacques to wonder at yet another mystery to him. He continued to look up at the vastly sprinkled sky, the giddy feeling as the mast dipped and rose and sketched a sweeping arc across it, and then slowly returned. There was a noise from for'ard as the carpenter came on deck, carrying a mug of weak coffee which he handed to the creature he had taken it upon himself to care for, from the time he knocked together the wood and canvas structure where he slept, and the great chair for the captain's cabin.

Mr Jackson took his hand from Jean-Jacques' sleeve. He said, with a certain pique, although covering it with a jest, 'I had no notion that you were our guest's personal servant.'

Any touch of irony escaped the carpenter. He said, 'I'm his friend, sir,' surprising himself that this was what he said. He explained he had made a drink for himself, as he did each evening, and hearing the movement on deck, had brought one up for the stranger. He did not remind Mr Jackson that he, after all, was the only member of the crew with permission to come close to him. For Captain Sharpe felt no obligation to explain his thinking to the crew. He knew that once they were back in England in what, God knows, might be twelve months' time or longer, the less that might be said about the giant—as their guest would at once be declared, a freak of nature—the better. Captain Sharpe alone, and young Jackson, would be the ones with knowledge of him.

With a curt nod, Mr Jackson turned. 'Wait for his mug, then go below,' he said as he left.

Jean-Jacques returned to making out the lines of the constellations. He and the smaller man seldom spoke. There was a rapport between them in which words took no great part. A trust, that was it, if he understood the word as he believed he did. He handed across his emptied mug. The carpenter within a few steps was taken by the night. *And yet I am not so close to any of them, as they believe. Is my thinking like theirs, or is it quite other? How am I to know?*

Whatever the novelty and satisfaction in what he so quickly grasped, a corresponding confusion lay beneath it like a sullen ache. It was in those times when he stood looking to the expanse of sea, or in the exhilaration of storms, that he craved to know more of what happened before those first memories that survived in him, that so troubled him. He saw himself as if reflected in some way by the agitation of the sea. Whatever he craved must be drawn from the turmoil he stood in the midst of.

The captain apprehended something of this. Yet a wall, in his own prosaic enough image, it was impossible to pass. For the sake of his return to London, at the end of his great if pointless voyage, he knew that his journal notes must continue to record details and impressions. For he would be the source, the first report, on what it was the *Dorothea*, in its Christian charity, had taken onboard. The first and final authority on how a huddled, near-naked, scarcely conscious, monstrous thing, was within months proving itself intelligent beyond expectation. Unfallen man, without concept of sin. Primitive beyond even that. A mind with no more awareness of the God who is Father to all, than he had of longitude before its logic was explained to him. 'Our inexplicable guest,' as he continued to write of him, putting distance between himself and Richard's fanciful naming of him.

The captain was comforted by the simple fact that there was no rush in needing to explain him; to define him more fulsomely than was patently the case, with his observant but puzzled notes. 'An extraordinary facility to accept anything to do with verifiable fact. A gift for spatial apprehension. Yet what difficulty—or so it seems to me—he has in grasping *temporal* reality. From what I can draw from him, his awareness of the past shades into a blur, and he confirms nothing of it. Wilfully or not I cannot be sure. And likewise of the future. It is, if I may put it so, rather like the sea we sail into. It is there, that is our one certainty. But to hazard more than that, seems not to interest him.' Another page with nothing on it but the captain's frustrated scrawl: 'The one question that, after all others, is so demanding of an answer. Is our guest truly some variant of ourselves, or, in a way that bewilders the mind, *sui generis*?' A line beneath, he had written in the crabbed hand of one who knew how valuable space was on a journal's page, 'God be in my heart, and in my understanding.' Whether this related to the lines he had written above or stood as a single and distant thought, that too might only be guessed at. As did, on that page again, the single word 'Lileth?' with its interrogatory mark. For the captain was erratically read in curious heretical by-ways. Did it not throw up the thought, fascinating if only because so dangerous, that another kind of man may have persisted through the ages? A covert stream. Another line of descent than our own.

So much changed onboard as the *Dorothea* sailed south and eastwards, towards the 'Great Continent' as the captain habitually called it. The usually taciturn carpenter said, as he handed Jean-Jacques a tin dish heaped with mash and fish, that they would sniff the land before it was in sight. He had shipped this way half a dozen years before, in a hellhole of a naval vessel, bringing reluctant Englishmen to punish themselves and the land they came to. And the sweetness of the trees, the carpenter said, like the floating charred logs he recalled seeing, far out he supposed from some river mouth, as if there to greet them. Others in the crew now went about their tasks with a kind of lightness that Jean-Jacques learned had to do with the fact that within a week or less, they would touch land, and the grog shops at Port Jackson were legendary. And the talk of women, too, whose full meaning escaped the guest. But so distinctly, the certainty of something new. They would be on the margin of a continent, the captain remarked to him, larger than the Europe they derived from. One's mind, he was told, could not be otherwise than buoyed at such a thought.

Jean-Jacques listened with the quietness that as always was taken for courtesy. He had no true understanding of what the captain might mean by all this. But he watched with pleasure as the pale stubbed finger moved down the margin of land on one of his charts. He liked to hear the details when Cook's own journals were read aloud. At times, Captain Sharpe said, there is an extraordinary likeness in the weather we experience here ourselves, and what the great seaman himself set down. A stroke of luck. A blessing. At times he would summon Mr Jackson and the guest to join him where he stood on the quarter deck, above one of his charts held down by pieces of Yorkshire rock he had brought with him on the journey for this purpose. His spyglass was in one hand. He would say, in a calm manner, but not bothered should his excitement show, 'Take a look at that sloping headland,' or, 'You see that bluff?' He would then say its name, given by Cook sailing within a few miles, surely, of where the *Dorothea* was positioned this very minute. He delighted especially if the conditions they sailed in coincided.

There was a duplicity, however, in Mr Jackson, that held him to saying little to the captain about what some would regard as a crazed notion of his own, one that grew more compelling now that they followed the coast of Terra Australis. With the vanity of one who considered himself a child of the Enlightenment, he did not for a moment see that what he would call the 'silliness' of his kinsman's expensive but harmless game of tracking the wake of Cook, was in fact less fanciful than the meagre case he had built for his own fame. To bring into the realm of science a creature that would stun the world of learning. A bird far larger than a standing man! That would make seem puny the scrawny but remarkable bird he had seen himself at Kew, its kind discovered a century back on the continent's other side, when it still went by the name New Holland. He had spoken of it to no one. But since his youthful days as a midshipman, he had carried a vivid memory. It was of a more than usually disgruntled sailor, one of the few crewmen who did not take his daily allowance of grog, one of the ardent Methodists some of the older men in the service loathed as undermining both the traditions and the manliness of the fleet.

Matthams, a Warwickshire man, had stood at the rail beside him and fired his own obsession. The fact that he had seen it. As a young man, on an American whaler out of New Bedford, but so far blown from its course that few believed they would return from the latitudes they were in; it seemed they had touched the southern corner of the terrifying world Cook had ventured into. Peaks he said like jagged teeth. Coves of black foliage and a sense of dreadful emptiness that would drive a man from his wits, should fortune cast him there. The whalers had found seals enough to kill, fish enough to last them a year. But each of them in fear for the days they spent there. They were landed by their captain to scour the vicious vegetation in the search for fruit, for whatever moved and might serve as meat that did not stink of fat and sea reek like the seals. When in a clearing of some sort they saw it. Not only as big as a man, Matthams swore, but a man's height doubled again. Its legs alone as thick as stanchions, its feathered body wide as an ox, its head at the end of its extended neck, beaked, tiny, stupid. By the time the bo'sun, the one man who carried a firearm, had the wit to raise his piece, agitation dragged his fire so wide the monstrous bird covered in a few enormous strides the small distance to the edge of tangled forest, and was gone. But three great toes, the informant remembered that, supported the towering bird. For he had examined the impressions that were left in the mud of where it had stood.

Matthams said most men thought him either mad or a liar if he spoke of it, and so was silent unless he met a man like Mr Jackson. He said, I would not even expect so much as a guinea, sir, were I to tell you the name of one of the men who was there beside me, and where to find him. A man who lives by the Bible and no more lie to you sir than strike our saviour on the cross. Mr Jackson had tracked him down in Bethnal Green. A dull man with a failing memory but who said yes, indeed, he would swear by his soul, that what Matthams said he would confirm. His wife drew the visiting young officer aside and said that in his dreams her husband at times seemed to see and fear the great bird he now spoke of. That he tied it to the Book of Revelations, but all that was beyond her. Her life had enough to occupy her without running to the ends of the earth, when a man to fix the latch on a loosened door was as much as she needed to thank Providence for.

There were years in which the lieutenant at times thought more about the men who had spoken to him. He consulted authorities on natural gigantism and guessed-at creatures, but most fell into the categories of mythical beings, or visions, or the reports of men who were patently given either to lies or a Cervantes-like gift for humorous exaggeration. The one or two learned or scientific men whom he sounded out thought he teased them in some droll way.

And yet. Now, with increasing distance from the equator, Richard Jackson felt how more and more they sailed from the certainties such men as himself might reasonably assume, into the hemisphere where the normal world no longer rang with certainty. Sharing so many hours of the day and evenings with his hero-worshipping kinsman, James Cook and those who sailed with him were spoken of almost as if acquaintances. The journals of Banks or early French explorers, also referred to daily, as some observation, some quirk of weather, a physical feature distantly noted, or even some passing thought in Captain Sharpe's mind were enough for some remark to be made or an opinion cited. There was something touching gaiety in the mood onboard that was not to be explained simply by the weather, the afternoon breezes, the crew's anticipation of days ashore. Surely much had to do with the two officers and the curious quirks of each mind? Although, Mr Jackson had made no more than a few passing references, until now, of a growing plan in his mind.

The captain smiled when he spoke of it, as he might at an enthusiastic boy. 'There, Richard, how ambition seems to swell the further we are from home!' But his relative's now touching on his own intentions provoked him to consider what until now he had so put off thinking of too closely. It would be as much as a year, who might tell, until it was an issue. But he thought more deeply of it now, as Richard sketched for him the kind of cage that would be required, and how a capture might be planned, and the fame at the end of it, imagine that, should such a prize reach the docks in London.

Captain Sharpe stood alone, watching the western skyline for the first rise of coast. No more than a day, and he would sail between the great red cliffs he had read of, at the entrance to Britain's newest, albeit notorious, colony. Already, great-winged gulls planed above the *Dorothea*. For so equable a man, a rushing sense of almost panic took hold of him. The feeling sharpened by his looking down on his guest, seated at such ease on one of the hatchways, his great hands spread across his thighs. He had spent the morning plaiting rope from strands so stiffened that a normal man would have cursed as he laboured at it. The captain leaned forward, grasping the rail in front of him, like a man catching his breath. Why had he not thought more of this before? His mind, more than usually during these past days, so taken with the records of Cook, that he had thought of little else, beyond those, and his duties as the ship's master. He supposed he had almost become attached to the guest, the uncouth figure now leaning back, his eyes closed, basking as any normal man might do in the late morning's warmth. Yet how much too, the captain thought, he had been given in return for his plucking him back to life. The guest had opened his mind to concepts that otherwise would not have come to him. Creation's capaciousness, how that had broadened for him. And yet not to have thought of this!

The captain called to a crewman hail-stoning the deck some yards' distance from him, to fetch the lieutenant.

'Sir?' Mr Jackson said.

The sailor had moved away, so the expected formality between the officers lapsed. The captain confessed frankly, 'I have made an error, Richard.' There was silence as he thought on how best to put it. He began by asking, lightly, was there anything his cousin might think of that was more likely to enrage the average tar than denying him the freedom of a port after months at sea? And when the lieutenant left unspoken so obvious an answer, he put another query. Was there a sailor on earth, whether in his cups or deadly sober, who does not boast of the wonders his travel has thrown his way? What he so liked others to think unique to him? He nodded towards the figure beneath them, its eyes still closed against the sun.

'Think of this,' the captain said. There would be talk of him in London while they themselves were still in the ices of the other Pole. The stories would be as different as the men who heard them in Sydney, versions already distant from those onboard who told them. What news would it be when the *Dorothea* itself returned? Their guest by then would not be current. He would by then be fodder for a freak show, not the great scientific wonder that he was. Was he not right in thinking that?

Captain Sharpe sensed the younger man's putting himself at a distance from any fringe of responsibility, and was disappointed. He said, 'I have a plausible solution.'

'Yes?' The lieutenant waited to be informed, rather than it seeming that he shared some part in it.

'Listen, then.' He would sail the *Dorothea* to within a mile of a landing quay, and anchor there. He then would announce to the crew, with genuine regret, that signalling from shore had just apprised of how things stood in the colony. That smallpox was ravaging the convicts, and that several deaths had been confirmed. He well knew the disappointment that ran through the crew. He assured them of double rations of grog for several days, once they had taken again to the Tasman Sea, and a further remuneration at journey's end. The men no doubt would mutter and fume, but they were good fellows, and as casks were broached the next day, they would again be in humour.

'And?' Mr Jackson queried.

'And the rest, Richard, is up to you.' For the lieutenant—rowed by the Swede, a man whose discretion could hold its own against the grave, and a Dutchman whose natural speech impediment was honed by so meagre a grasp of English few understood him—would then be the one man to go ashore. The pinnace would stand off a hundred yards until Lieutenant Jackson had purchased what was needed. He would signal the ship's boat to return, which would be loaded, and another small craft, and the men to row it, hired from the providores, to ferry further supplies of fresh produce, the usual tack of a crew's diet, as well as fowls and several small pigs. He would have explained that some unidentified illness, which was not a deadly affliction but certainly one not wanted in the town of military health and Britain's bad seed, was like a fire, the way it had spread through the ship. The chandler's craft would be brought alongside the *Dorothea*, and the unloading supervised by the captain himself. No loose talk of freakish human cargo, or the fever itself, would have the opportunity to occur.

In the few hours he spent on the hot and wretchedly fetid waterfront, Mr Jackson was unimpressed with the areas set off for part encampment, part prison, before he walked a higher street of more or less decent structures, and a handsome church. Even, between other places of commerce and bartering, a small shop with shelved books and papers arranged in racks, as they might have been at home. The only customers were several women. One was a mother with two young daughters, who struck him as something of an apparition in their white frocks, their coloured ribbons. Young Jackson's head reeled for a moment with the suddenness of so much that took him back to what shipboard life deprived one of. The quick scent of jasmine water, was it, as the woman passed close by him?

Again, as if this were something he might do daily at home, he inspected the dates on the various news sheets and papers, and took up several London papers as were there in front of him. He fell upon copies of the *Edinburgh Review*. A mildly spoken assistant took them and made a parcel, binding them firmly with twine. He said as he handed them to the lieutenant, 'News is only old, sir, if we were aware of it beforehand.' There was something not quite cowering about the man, but watchful, expectant. He spoke almost as an equal, yet insistently polite. Mr Jackson enjoyed the few minutes they spoke together. He wondered if the man was one of those who had come in chains and worked his way to some kind of pardon. He liked to think so. When he asked, from curiosity, if the shelved books might include a copy of Rousseau, the other man's clear blue eyes held his own directly as he smiled and said, without seeming too bothered whether the women overheard him, 'The man I work for, the one who chooses the books. He does not think such reading is what we need.'

Quite what the man meant by his remark, or for that matter, by the quick intense glance he directed to the lieutenant, was not easy to guess. In a better world, Richard Jackson felt they might indeed have more to talk of together. But his attention was taken then by one of the women among the customers, a tall serious widow, he guessed, from the dark clothes she wore. She held a dark-covered book in her hand. A strange title, which she turned towards him, and beneath, a woman's name. She said, with a directness that surprised him, 'A detestable book, which I could not put down. Even though it runs to three volumes.'

Mr Jackson laughed at the unexpectedness of it. 'One you obviously recommend? I'm not greatly attracted to fiction, to be honest with you.'

'It calls itself a novel,' the woman said. 'You may not believe so by the end.'

Mr Jackson bowed in a manner he had had no call for these many months. 'With that then in its favour,' he told her. He bought the book, but doubted he would read it. It was true that novels seldom appealed to him. He had noticed, though, that when the captain took up something other than his hero's *Journals*, or other accounts of discovery, the opening up of seas and the fame of previously unrecorded landfalls, it was often the enormously long fiction by Fielding that he held. A name he knew without interest enough to open for himself.

'Human nature,' Captain Sharpe had answered him, when once Mr Jackson had asked whether it was the story he read for in these volumes, or the pleasure he took in the writing. Or 'the depiction of manners'; wasn't that a phrase he had heard in defence of novels? 'What we may have failed to observe for ourselves,' the captain said, 'but we may be the better for knowing. One mind enlarged by the fineness of another.'

So the large packet of newspapers, the *Edinburgh Review*, and the novel with its curious title and a woman's name beneath it, all placed in a canvas sack that the lieutenant carried with him as he returned to the warehouse whose men were loading the provisions he had bought. He stood at the doorway facing the broad Quay, conversing with the owner, whose cockney accent at first had startled him. As they spoke a stout man wearing a faded military jacket approached them, but limping, and clearly beyond service. He held by a length of chain a dog so huge one instinctively stepped back. A finely muscled body, handsome even, but a repellent head. And Mr Jackson excited as he looked at it—an idea not forming in his mind but there, complete, before the man and his charge were level with him and the chandler he spoke with. The lieutenant asked, 'It tracks? It must be to track?'

The stout man laughed as if he were teased. 'Well, he's a land killer, if that's what you're asking. He's no sea-dog, like.' He grinned at his joke. Then, in a tone that seemed to carry on his good humour, 'A preference for blacks, given the chance. I've seen him bring down three in an afternoon.'

'But tractable?' Mr Jackson asked. 'To a master?'

'Supposing he takes a shine to him. I've never tried to read his mind.'

The businessman put in, 'Christ help the wrong person, if it comes to that.' He and the animal's owner laughing together.

'Five guineas then,' Mr Jackson said.

'Six.' The price absurdly high, as if its owner made another of his jokes.

'Done, then.'

The three crossed the Quay to where the *Dorothea*'s boat lay loaded, waiting to return. The man who had made his sale winked. 'Keep his gob bound up, like. He's used to men who don't bother him. And just one who rules.'

The officer who had bought him nodded. 'I hear you,' he said.

'Then you'll find him good at what he does.'

Before the men rowed off Mr Jackson called, 'He has a name?'

'Dog does him,' the man answered him.

As the boat came alongside its ship, Captain Sharpe understood at once the tableau he looked down on: Richard standing, and the huge shape motionless beside him, its mouth in a metal grating. Ferox, the captain would have named him. But his kinsman told him it had never been other than what the man in his military jacket had said.

'So Dog he is,' the captain smiled. Part, no doubt, of the young man's plan.

That evening, Jean-Jacques was not invited to join them. The two men sat in silence, reading, although each distracted, too, by how close they were to what lay ahead. For the captain, the real satisfaction he would take was in anchoring where Cook had shipped over for a week, almost exactly thirty years back to the day; for the lieutenant, it was in what may have been a pipe-dream, he quite saw that, but then again it might not. The perversity of freedom, should a man take the courage to accept it.

In melodramatic terms, or those of romantic fiction, the *Dorothea* may as well have run aground on a jagged reef, or smashed against the base of a cliff, as have made its duplicitous entrance into Port Jackson, flung its net of lies, and continued on, sailing into latitudes that excited the ship's captain as lewd prints might stir a lecherous mind, or Wesley's hymns a field of factory workers gathering in the spirit's sheaves.

The change that came over the *Dorothea* was of a kind that alters men forever. To pursue the fervid imagery of a preacher, the skies they lived beneath were changed; their spirit took on a stain that only a divine act might erase. Or so it might seem as Captain Sharpe's usual equanimity of mind withered within days. When the shock came, nothing was untouched by it.

Mr Jackson was on the quarterdeck, discussing the set of sails with the mate, when he heard a shout of a kind he had not heard before, from the captain's quarters. A southerly was coming upon them suddenly, but nothing that was not in the normal run of seamanship. Jean-Jacques stood not far off, listening with interest, as he always did, to the business and detail of how a ship was handled and prepared. The deck was busy with several men assisting the carpenter with the making of stalls for the pigs and cages for the poultry. Several others of the crew sat cross-legged on the deck, repairing and checking sails. For once the seas mounted and the glass fell, as they had been told to expect, there would be little enough time for casual tasks.

There was a general sense of satisfaction among the men, and for most of them, the prospect of sailing further south than as yet they had ventured. And now as well, Mr Jackson spoke openly about the prize he hoped they would assist him in attempting to possess, once they were in the fjords and harbours which the captain also so anticipated. Mr Jackson showed them drawings he had done of what he hoped to see with his own eyes. The men joked about the quest, even as they took it seriously, and the lieutenant fired them with a purse of ten guineas for the first man to call and confirm a sighting. Already there were discussions of how such things might be done, but the suggestions were wild enough, as none had ever attempted such a thing. Spreading nets across tracks, digging pits the creature might fall into, setting variants of traps used for country pests. Firearms were only a last resort, for the object of the hunt was a perfect specimen, even if dead. But across all this, at the shout from the captain's cabin those close enough to hear it looked fearfully at each other. Captains who commanded respect were not given to bawling out. And none of those onboard had sailed under one they respected more.

The lieutenant stood shocked as he found the captain slumped at his desk, his florid complexion paled, as if the pained face he observed were that of another man.

'There is nothing wrong with me, man, for Christ's sake!' That too perhaps the first time blasphemy had crossed his lips. Jackson poured a deep shot of brandy from the locker where medical supplies were kept. The captain tilted the glass high then banged it on the board in front of him to be refilled. This time Mr Jackson took a glass himself.

He sat upright and eased himself back, straightening his shoulders. He said, 'We have no notion, Richard, of what we have onboard.' He touched one of the volumes in front of him, where it lay opened at the final pages. 'We give succour to evil.' His language became more theatrical, so Mr Jackson thought, unfamiliar as he was with the cadences of theology and commitment.

'Tell me,' the lieutenant said. 'Explain it to me simply, Francis.'

'All you need,' Captain Sharpe said, 'is to confirm what our eyes have seen.' He paused and laughed with an hysterical lift to his voice. 'Waiting for us to rescue him!'

Jackson took the book as the captain directed him. He turned to the title page. 'A woman,' he said.

'None the less believable for that.'

'I was not impugning, Francis,' Mr Jackson said.

The captain turned the glass in his hand. He said, 'That old apophthegm we are quick to affix to others and seldom to ourselves. "Pride goeth before a fall."'

'You cannot with any justice apply that to yourself.'

'A hard heart makes a man detestable. But a gullible one?' Again, the captain's dismissive laughter at himself. 'One of those fools Dante speaks of.'

'That I wouldn't know.'

A long pause as Jackson leafed through the account of what man alone had made. He repeated the title on the cover. 'The names these imaginative women think of. The way they tell us fact by another name.'

He sat, and it was some hours before he spoke again. With that gift senior officers so often have, the glasses Captain Sharpe drank as he watched young Jackson read served to clear his mind. When the lieutenant closed the book and rested it on his knee, he felt the pang of being chastened in his optimism for what humanity might one day be. The heavy irony striking him as he raised his eyes and caught the painting. Blue-veiled Mary with a vacant book lying opened in front of her, her attention on the eternal verity of what was yet to be written.

The captain now spoke in a more controlled voice, once

again the man accustomed to order, to definite decisions, whatever the touch of craziness Jackson never doubted was also part of his temperament. There was a challenge unlike any other his career had faced him with. What was to be done with a creature now revealed to be as morally depraved as he was, in every aspect a thing beyond nature? He said, 'You have now read for yourself what he has done, how he comes to exist. A charnel house. A beast cobbled from corpses and the over-reaching of science.'

Jackson was shaken by what he had read. He waved aside the offer to refill his glass. He asked, 'And so? What now?'

'Surely it would be a reasonable instinct to destroy the creature. Only I fear that too.' When the younger man said nothing to that, Francis Sharpe went on, 'Whatever the circumstances, he is a living being.'

'We kill without scruple for our country's sake,' Jackson said. 'Captains hang men at sea when discipline demands.' He spoke more from irritation than principle. It pained him to see his relative so racked. His own thoughts moved quickly, his conscience less troubled by scruple. Several notions jostled together. In recent weeks, as he elaborated his own no longer rational plans for future fame, the creature took a central part in what he planned. He accepted—how could he not—the mockery of the enlightened name he had given it. But now the added perversity in continuing to speak of him as Jean-Jacques. Neither men for a second took in the absurdity of Mr Jackson's saying, 'The advantage we always have in controlling him, Francis. It is not manacles and chains that we must use in restraining him, but our own rational thought.'

'Both,' the captain said. 'It will come to both.' He stood gazing through the small square of glass to what was no more than an evening blur of mingling sea and sky, his fingers playing and knotting behind his back.

The lieutenant said, 'The first thing I would observe is that while we are the only two who know what the book reveals, nothing onboard has altered by a jot, apart from the burden we share.'

The captain said nothing, the signal that he expected his lieutenant to continue, as he did. 'So long as we behave in what the men, and our guest too especially, think is our accustomed manner, then nothing has changed.'

An exasperated clearing of his throat, as Captain Sharpe turned and again sat behind his desk. An irritating image coming to mind of Dorothea, on one of her melancholy days, sitting with her tabby on her knee, content to stroke it for an hour at a time. Thinking it as he saw young Jackson with the last volume balanced on the knee of his crossed leg, his palm moving across its cover with an almost tender brushing.

'How you can bear the sight of it,' the captain said.

Mr Jackson placed the book on the floor by his chair. He repeated, 'He is no threat to us at the moment. That is all I claim.'

The captain's voice rising as he said, 'The moment is not a concept that carries force, Richard. We know what the creature does, and does on impulse. A creature who has killed men, children. Dear God, what else do we need to know of him to know we may indeed be next!'

Mr Jackson said, 'It is not so difficult a thing to come up behind a man with a pistol. If one is left with no other choice.' Yet knowing as he said it, his cousin would not bring himself to that. For neither needed to spell out such other complications as the testimony of the crew that there was no hint of mutiny; that, monster as he might appear, the creature taken onboard had behaved with civility, had worked to save a man's life, had been entertained evening after evening, displaying nothing but courtesy and gratitude. And then to shoot him in cold blood?

'There is the book,' the captain said.

'Yes, there is the book, and its evidence is damning. But to prove absolutely our creature was that? You know them yourself, Francis, the intricacies of the law. The muddled testimony of common men. The temperament, even that, of who judges whom on a particular day. The punishment that faces a man whose judgement errs in such in affairs.'

Mr Jackson knew his words harried the captain to an even more despondent mood.

'While he sits on the deck this very moment.'

'So long as he is ignorant, we are safe.'

II

Thoughts came to him randomly rather than in the straight lines, the sequences, that the captain and Mr Jackson seemed to have in mind when they spoke of 'thinking'. He remembered a child he had seen in Switzerland, before the other events he tried always to put from his mind. It sat playing with flat coloured pieces of wood, and moved them about, until what had looked no more than scraps formed a picture. The little girl had clapped her hands, although there was no one nearby to see what she had done. He had taken a strange delight in watching her. So his own thoughts now, separate and unrelated and yet at times, so unexpectedly, a pattern to them which had not been there the evening before. But that too, so suddenly gone, as if his mind once more was the slate that Mr Jackson had spoken of early on; our minds are slates, he had said, until the lines we mark on them come to carry a sense of their own. The lines still there but their meanings a tangle of confusion these last few days. The change as if a great blast had swept against the craft they sailed in; a huge hand had turned the ship completely, so that it now headed away from where it sailed towards, and the instruments that guided it ran contrary to their purpose. *For all the closeness I was to both of them, both of them, the further off I now stand.*

What might the captain and his young lieutenant now write of him in their fat journals? The comfort there had been, some evenings, when the three sat in silence in the master's cabin, and he had leaned his head back against the panelled wall, feeling the thrum of the ship coursing through the wood and into his veins. The sound of their writing pleased him, the soft click of the quills clipping the edge of the ink-horns, the scratching of the nibs as they wrote his replies to their various questions, or at times let their pens, like little wings, fly across the paper of their journals, and the sound of a fresh page turned, and nothing else but the captain's soft grunt from time to time as something he wrote pleased him. But such things already in that other life, before the ship's boat had rowed into the new town, and the world turned by the time Mr Jackson returned with the book in which Mary's writing so enraged the captain. From then on, so little understood. The scribbled knots on the slate which he must think of, if he thought of his own mind. While in the cabin with its marvellous charts, its instruments for displaying the motions of the planets, for assessing time on the world's other side, or the currents of the ocean that bore them, the two officers argued, one with a passion the other thought deranged, while Mr Jackson's motives were clear to himself only because he so easily accepted his own lie. When the older man used such terms as 'the seat of human affections', which his cousin felt only scorn for, as he did for 'unnatural' and 'the reality of sin', Mr Jackson said, impatiently, 'Humanity, Francis, is whatever comes into the realm of what we choose to admit.'

'Christ help us all then!' Captain Sharpe said quietly. Far more clearly than his young kinsman did, he saw beyond the officer facing him and his cheerful rhetoric. He saw for a moment of dreadful clarity a vision that appalled him, and that in half a century's time would drive a grandson to suicide from a church spire, and so many others to despair, or worse—to the ruthlessness of science, to morality shucked off like ancient rags. For the lieutenant, it was a memory of things so recent that troubled him.

Before Sydney, before the blurred first glimpsing of the coast of Australia, before the distant smoky villages within sight for several days as the startlingly green islands off Indonesia drifted past, 'the first occasion', as a cleric indeed might choose to put it. Had such things been thought proper for committing in his journal, Mr Jackson may well have entered them, in the form of questions he put to himself and frankly answered.

Where? In the makeshift shelter the carpenter had knocked together for him soon after he was taken from the ice.

When? In the hours of darkness, between watches, but as there is no such thing onboard to match what is known as privacy on shore, one must add, *as circumstances might allow.*

Why? To answer that would wrench one into the mires of disagreement where the captain and the lieutenant amiably confronted one tradition with another, one view of man with its opposite, so for the sake of peace they 'left it there', as the captain liked to say.

Then begin at the beginning. The words which may have mattered at the time. Not long before the trade winds entered into the ship's log. Kindness and curiosity. By now Jean-Jacques quite understood the meaning of both words, and their importance to the men who had befriended him. Yet the change too, which he was quick to pick up on, when one evening, after their shared hours with the captain, the lieutenant, for the first time, addressed him in his other tongue. Simply, and yet the feeling of something new between them. Mr Jackson suddenly there, a block of darkness against the lighter oblong of the entrance to the hut. *'Pardon, mon ami. Excusez-moi.'*

It was not unusual for the younger officer to wish the guest goodnight as he made his final round of the ship, spoke briefly with the man on watch, and checked below decks where the crew heaved or snored or lay silent in their canvas hoops. Yet tonight, so Jean-Jacques thought, Mr Jackson seemed ill at ease. Earlier he had complained of a returning ache in his shoulder, from a brawl when he was first at sea. He now paused as he stood above Jean-Jacques, who lay on the hut's floor. He then said, his voice tight, but his speech as quick as if he were giving orders, again in his own language, 'Those measurements I have taken before, I fear are not accurate as I had hoped. So if I may?'

'You will be measuring the dark,' Jean-Jacques said. A rare sense of amusement touching him. But Mr Jackson seemed not to share it with him. He knelt and lifted from the distorted yet impressive body the light garment he wore at night, seemingly indifferent to the temperature that so obviously meant more to all others onboard.

'The length of one thigh,' Mr Jackson said. 'It seems not to match the other as squarely as I had thought.' The darkness and the unseen movement of his hands did not strike Jean-Jacques as inconsistent with those earlier occasions, when a marked tape had run across his neck and shoulders, his biceps, his calves. But now, when Mr Jackson's fingers moved across him once his shirt had been removed, Jean-Jacques felt his body stirred in a manner he did not expect, his mind alert to this new sensation. Whatever the darkness, he noted the change in the officer's breathing, a tautness that he imagined must this moment alter the other's face, as it was lowered and laid against his stomach. Mr Jackson's fist now moving rapidly, Jean-Jacques own rasped breath as if beyond his control. Unable to comprehend more than a sense of swirling intensity, racking him beyond delight, until the officer's saying softly, his mouth close enough to press wetly against his ear, 'For shame!' The lieutenant then gone without further words, the sound of his treading softly towards the stern.

Jean-Jacques lay long without sleeping. For the first time the word 'soothed' in his mind, using it of the gentle rising and dipping of the sea. He wondered at what had just occurred. At how or where it took its place among the countless other things he had learned since his own first sighting of the ship, small and strangely living, like a distant black insect, between the glaring blocks of ice. What to make of what he had so felt exalted by, and then so desolate once it had concluded with Mr Jackson's abrupt leaving.

Did this or something similar occur at other times?
Oh yes.
Did Mr Jackson refer to such at other times?
Oh no.

After such times Jean-Jacques would lie, as he did now, several days south from Sydney, watching as the few stars in the hut's open entrance were taken by the lightened sky. How clearly he had believed his understanding grew, but now the tangled rigging he took his own mind to be. Where did this experience of one man's flesh against another's take its place among those other gifts that had been explained to him? The words like liberty, like human rights and the dignity of man? Where did such an act as he had just lived through, that both elated and depressed him, take its place?

Now the dreadful weight of Mary's book, when the lieutenant quietly spoke of it, against his captain's orders. Mr Jackson in fact was excited, as much as appalled, by what he had read. His enquiring mind made its notes on what he observed, attentive to how the miscreant heard such details of himself. 'She wrote that?' Jean-Jacques would sometimes say. From the beginning she was making him into what he was. He raised his arm and rested it along the hard cordage that ran beneath his forehead. Tears too. These were new to him. The taste of the sea. Of himself.

The captain, halfway across the Tasman, was struck down with a fever that confined him to his cabin. The duties of command fell to his younger relative, who was not a man with a natural gift for exercising authority, too conscious of himself as distinct from the uniform he wore. Captain Sharpe lay in bed, believing a strong emetic and medicinal brandy would restore him to his usual florid health. When he appeared again on deck, he was in fact pale and without the briskness his men admired in him. Only Mr Jackson might guess that it was more the captain's mind than anything physic might attend to. But once he was well enough to move again amongst them, a discomfort spread among the crew. Too much that was beyond their understanding was taking place. The feeling encouraged throughout most of the journey—that to call at the fjords where Cook himself had laid over was a privilege to celebrate—seemed blighted by an uneasiness, but with nothing more substantial to account for it. And there was the dog, which for several of the men seemed to represent their new indefinable fear.

The outsized skulking creature, standing waist high or higher to most of those onboard, its hair the colour of pooled urine, endeared itself to no one. It snarled and fanged at any who approached it. Yet if the ship's grotesque guest stood anywhere near its chained area, it took on a quietness not otherwise there. Even the boy from the galley, delegated to feed it, pushed its tin dish of slops towards it with a length of wood and edged it back towards him when emptied. Jean-Jacques gave no hint of caring for the dog so much as permitting it to stand beside him. Both seemed indifferent to everything but themselves.

But Captain Sharpe, one afternoon during his illness, had done an extraordinary thing. He insisted that the monster, as the guest was now fixed in his mind, be brought into his cabin to sit in the ungainly chair where he had taken his place on the evenings when the officers had observed and noted and spoken to him, gifting him 'concepts' as they named them, the notions and ideas of civilised men. This time, one of the mates, holding a firearm, was told to stand with his back against the door and instructed not to hesitate in firing should the least incident occur.

It was beyond Mr Jackson's guessing, whatever it was that prompted the captain to such a tableau. Some overhang, surely, from the old religion, a mind at ease with images rather than ideas. Nothing was said in the cabin, which now seemed so much smaller. The ship's master lay with his legs propped on a stool, covered by a blanket brought from his bed in its adjoining alcove, a spread of double-knitted squares made by his distant wife. For most of the afternoon he slept, but at times would rouse with a sudden shaking of his shoulders and stare at the features of the creature facing him. As though attempting to comprehend its evil—was that it, Mr Jackson wondered? In some way to pit himself against it? An effort to take in with understanding, rather than just disgust, this shock that had come to him—the incarnation of evil, which up until now was more like something he had heard or merely read of? As close, and yet as incomprehensible as this, the spit-coloured eyes looking back into his own with their vile mildness. *Sweet Jesus!*

The captain went over in his mind the atrocities the book had brought to him, the depravity that clawed so deeply. One event after another forcing itself so vividly, the lone figure against the Alps, the murdered child, the stain of his presence from one page to the next. There came a muffled clink as the crewman shifted his position at the door. Captain Sharpe jolted from his dozing. The mate said quietly, 'Everything correct, sir.'

The captain reached for the glass he drank from. His earlier fear, when the fever shook him, had now left him. Even his daily reading of Cook's journals had been put aside. It was as if his long and unwitting kindness to the rescued creature had drained him of vitality, and even husked his beliefs. What he did not speak of to his lieutenant, and was so tangled by in his thoughts, was how best—how at all!—to resolve a decision he knew he must come to. What he feared must draw him close to a determining error of his own. He had hoped that to have the creature facing him so directly, to close his eyes and again open them to what he feared most and least understood, would in some way shake him into calling reality by its new name. And yet the risk of that! On one occasion he dreamed that he himself, like that maimed and distant shape, attempted to find purchase on a rocking slab of ice. He woke in sweat the lieutenant dabbed from him with a dampened cloth. The creature watching him with its neutral eyes. But while the captain slept again, Jean-Jacques looked only at the wall behind the captain. He sat there, unmoving, as if he and the roughly hewn chair were hacked from the same block. Or so the man who guarded him thought, as the light at the cabin's windows dimmed.

Throughout the afternoon the giant, as many of the crew still referred to him, seemed only to attend to the painted image of Mother Mary, as so early on in their voyaging the captain had identified her. A name of course meaning so much less until Port Jackson, when all things were made clear. The book of himself. At last, to know that he, as all things, became true again in print. And what may not be true, that too. For if a thing is written it is understood. What he had endured, the force of events that drove him as if before a whip, such things as she had told it. And so he sat for those several hours, careful not to move or creak the timbers of his chair and disturb in any way the captain who had been his friend and surely would be so again. As Mr Jackson had remained. For against all oaths he may have sworn to his captain, he passed on to Jean-Jacques so much of what the book had said. What Mary had written of him. A thing of fear, and yet surely dear to her, that she wrote so much? He longed for things to be as they were before, not to have changed, as they so suddenly had done.

For the next three days the wind blew sharply offshore. Then rough seas, the sighting of whales, an albatross landing on deck that terrified those in the crew moved by signs and stories. The first glimpses of the other land were black patches between low cloud, and only on the final evening did the clouds rise enough to show the stark uplifting to the east, its peaks partly obscured by the shore seeming to rise directly from the sea into great slabs of darkness, a sense of desolation that fretted all onboard, some of whom were imagining palms, or sky-scraping peaks. All, that is, apart from Captain Sharpe, who knew by heart the words his hero had written on entering the Sound the *Dorothea* would enter at first light. And the fancy his young kinsman carried as a sense of mission, the search that already in his imagining assured him of modest fame at least. To bring back, living and unbelievable until sight confirmed it, the creature that had eluded even the great Banks, a thing that common sense itself would have no part of.

Once the anchor was cast as close as possible to where Captain Sharpe believed his great predecessor had decided on, men leaned on the railings, or climbed in the tracery of rigging, their mood a mix of elation and despondency. Few would ever have thought possible a land this far from England, or the burden of distance that came with thinking so. Yet as well, within the same few minutes, they might feel an awe of a kind unlike anything they had known, the 'sublimity', as Captain Sharpe was heard to say, of where the *Dorothea* lay.

Jean-Jacques stood in the chained-off area of the deck, the mastiff beside him, its leash wrapped round the great fist of the one other creature it acknowledged or was subdued by. A now middle-aged man who had known animals in his younger years, and who kept his distance from the massive animal spoken of among the crew simply as Dog, pondered, as the officers had done, on what it was that so drew these figures together; if not a liking for each other, it was at least a tolerance that united them. He watched the two beings who seemed to him so beyond any dispensation of the Lord. Their closeness, he guessed, drew on the certainty, the loneliness, at the core of each. The rescued stranger with the foreign name the officers had given him may have impressed the crew with his apparent quietness, his usefulness in such labours as bearing the weight of a collapsed spar while a wounded seaman—a youngster most certainly killed at any other time—was lifted from beneath it. But better surely to keep the stranger at a distance, to glance downwards or to the side when on occasion he addressed them with some simple greeting, an expelling of air that rasped above their heads. The freakish man and the dog beside him, immobile, yet the sense given out from each of turmoil in repose.

The ship swayed slightly at what seemed less than a mile from the beachless shore, unless you considered occasional areas of strewn stone and fanned out slips of rock that might serve as landing places should one of the boats be sent ashore. Dark stunted growth almost to the shoreline and, on the slopes above, thicker and taller trees without the varied softness of European woods. The towering hills rose steeply. For all that might be said of the word the captain had used of it, confronted with such scale and such emptiness the human mind might feel not so much exalted as diminished. Again, only Captain Sharpe, with his store of fact and detail not only from Cook's writing but from other recorders of such voyaging as well, seemed undaunted by the place, by the vast sheet of gloom that came down on it within minutes, as a heavy front of rain poured across the slopes towards them, insistent, drenching, a cape of bitter cold hauled across the fjord. The crew quickly reaching for their pea-jackets and tarred canvas vests and wool-lined caps.

The captain and Mr Jackson stood in the alcove beneath the aft deck. A heavy sense of what the lieutenant suddenly conceded as possible fantasy came down on him, so that for a few moments he missed the words that the captain addressed to him. Four days, he was saying. Four days in which one party of men would go to find an adequate spar to replace the recently fractured one, the same duration he would allow for the younger man to find traces, at least, of the prey he was obsessed with. As they spoke the sound of waterfalls broke in on them, columns of descending water, thin strips of glittering white there against the dark perpendicular cliff face, as channels from the persisting downpour found the grooves and gutterings of rock. Some fell directly into the black spread of the fjord beneath them; others were held high or blown wide in veils by crossing winds.

After the storm another stillness, apart from the distant impacting falls on the steel-coloured water, fell across the enormous spaces. The two officers moved from beneath the shelter of the aft deck. The men were summoned, and the captain spoke to them in a voice there was no more need to raise than if they attended within a room. These were their instructions for the coming days, the time he allotted them to the two tasks he spoke of. No more than that, he said, fearing that closer to the Pole might test them more severely, should summer turn earlier than he hoped. One party of a dozen men would serve under Evans, the first mate, to find and shape a replacement for the ship's damaged spar. The group would include skilled workmen, the strongest for the axe work and the hauling. The carpenter, he reminded them, was skilled at setting bones, at drawing together the sides of gashes, even severing limbs. Thank God, as Captain Sharpe reminded the men, there had been little call on him so far on their journey. He led them now, as he was likely to do at such summonings, in the Lord's Prayer. For whatever intention, he said, that pleased a higher power to assist them.

Another six were assigned to the lieutenant, for what the captain now more certainly thought a pointless hunt. Yet he felt he owed him that. The young man had so far served well on a voyage most seamen would regard as both vanity and folly. A persisting vein of realism allowed Francis Sharpe to acknowledge it. Yes, he owed his kinsman loyalty. He spoke dutifully rather than with conviction, humouring his cousin, as he kept his word. And so Mr Jackson chose the men he would take with him, each of them roused to his own obsession. Two brothers from Devonshire, a stolid Scot, the ship's smithy, a German who in his past had served with Yorkshiremen who had been under Captain Sharpe's command since their taking to the sea as youths. A boy from the galley, to provide their meals and keep the camp. Men with certainty the great bird was there for them to track. And all, including the lieutenant himself, not so much speaking of it aloud but convinced within themselves that it was in the giant, and Dog, that finally their strength must lie.

One of the ship's boats made several trips between the patch of chosen shore, and the *Dorothea*. Canvases were ferried across for the shelters the men would build, once their struts and supports had been axed and trimmed. Then the sacks of food, although it was assumed fish would be easy enough to come by in the bays; the skillets and pots and plates and mugs the boy would need; the firearms and machetes, the coiled extensive ropes that would hold the captured prey, the fetters and chains that might be called for, for its strength may indeed be greater than mere ropes might hold; and the iron bars, the height of a man, whose uses might range from belaying on rough slopes to whatever emergencies might come in moving or confining something whose dimensions could only be guessed.

The terrain proved from the start more challenging than Mr Jackson expected. Not only the height of the country they would enter, but its appalling extensiveness. What inroads might they make in the few days the captain had given them? How hope to find a creature that no man yet had accurately described, the kind of thing which might yet turn out to be no more than the fantastical imagined beings placed on maps for places not yet known? From the first high peak the party achieved on the first day's exploring, they saw the rise of further mountain chains, horizons fading into a blue haze, an expanse as vast as several English counties. While to make one's way forward through the interlocking tangle of the lower forest, the tearing and whipping thrash of the packed growth, at times demanded hours to progress a few chains. The party arrived back to the shoreline camp in near darkness, the men exhausted and sore. Even with breaking out a generous allowance of rum, Mr Jackson's attempt to cheer his men was little more compelling than a schoolmaster's with a despondent class, as he said to them, 'If it was to be easy, men, we need not have come this far to prove it.'

The lieutenant's plan had been to confine his search to the slopes and heights within a few hours climbing from the shores of the fjord. He reasoned that the few reports and stories he had heard of the creature they hunted must indeed have been seen by men not far from the shore, or on the closer slopes. None of the witnesses would have been so much as half as far as they had covered that day, none within an hour of the waterline, at most. None of his men offered the opinion that it may not have been country like this at all that the rumours of the great bird came from. It was a country as Cook had shown, with a long ambling coastline. But no, 'deep in the south', the rare reports of sightings always began. Ships carried off-course. Men isolated and then found. The rumoured testimony of the dead. When hard evidence is rare, possibility is what we must trust. Mr Jackson's belief that he worked by rational calculation more tested than he knew.

The direction the next day took, however, was determined by sheer luck as he was obliged to call it, not having the captain's notion of providence to fall back on. The German sail-maker, whose fetish for cleanliness in itself put something of space between himself and his fellow crewmen, had swum round at first light to a small neighbouring inlet. In walking its narrow strip of sand, he had noticed what seemed, surely, like the beginnings of a track. Dog's subsequent lunging forward must surely mean a scent of some kind had been confirmed? Mr Jackson was excited, a schoolboy with an unexpected but longed-for gift. That, he said, is where the day's search would begin. For the first hours they followed the ascending Dog, and the huge figure that controlled it. The lieutenant followed immediately behind, carrying a long, finely twined rope looped across his shoulder, and two firing pieces in his leather belt. One of the brothers behind him wore two hatchets hanging from his belt, and another in his hand. He claimed to have helped clear entire plantations in the Indies. The second mate, with his reputation for near perfect accuracy, was third in line, a long-barrelled rifle slanted across his chest. The German walked ahead of the lieutenant, his muscular arm flailing with a machete when branches, or a species of barbed vine spread across it. How else could this appearing then disappearing narrow stretch of hardened earth, Mr Jackson asked, be described as anything other than a track? They had seen nothing like it in the previous day's reconnoitring. When Reuben turned to say that he was yet to be convinced, sir—how could there be such growth at certain places, and a swung iron blade needed to hack at it in others?—the lieutenant, more like an enthused schoolboy, said that even a half track was closer to a track than to its not being one. The men laughed. Their good humour buoyed them as the sun rose higher and they quickly sweated. The respite from the routines of ship life gifted them too with an expanding sense of themselves as adventurers.

Back onboard the *Dorothea*, with the absence of the one other educated man ashore, and the monster blessedly out of sight or hearing, the captain drew further into himself. Physically, the fever had diminished him. The burden of what he had learned after provisioning at Port Jackson compressed his normal faith-sustained good spirits into constant anxiety. He spoke, almost as an aging teacher might, to the youngsters on watch. He considered how on future voyaging, perhaps, the slow drag of days when weather was calm and immediate demands were few, might be the time to teach such lads to read more attentively than they did, even to calculate elementary problems.

Francis Sharpe walked the quarter-deck. As the dales came to mind, he felt their distance more sharply than he had known in all his years at sea. He wrote long pages affectionately to his wife. God knows when or if his letter might be held by her, at the high bow window with its fall of morning light. He found, without shame, that he could lie to her without scruple, if her happiness were the result. He told her of the pleasure of visiting England's freshest outpost in Sydney, the descriptions he had cribbed from Richard. He gave a close account of what had not taken place, and the great blank, almost like a continent itself, where he said nothing of the creature that so absurdly had delighted him, and now so deeply tormented. That soon enough he would leave in this exquisite desert, washing his hands of him, freed from regret. He wrote of an elation he felt not a splinter of, at anchoring where his greatest countryman had taken in what he too looked out to now in its grand intimidation. He wrote, more truthfully, for God to keep her, his precious wife, and spare her distress of any kind. He put down his quill and sprinkled across the still wet ink the fine sand from its phial. He looked at the stained oak panelling of what he might as well call home as anywhere, at the Italian painting that gave such meagre comfort. An absurd thought, he knew, but it was as if the other's gaze, to which he had so often returned as they sat on those evenings that may as well have been a century back, had drained the image of the beauty and the solace which had once been his own.

He folded the pages of his letter. The comfort that might be drawn from a narrative of lies. The dreadful irony striking him that Dorothea, distant, ailing, would draw her own happiness from those fabrications, as perhaps she had seldom done from the truth he had offered her across so many years.

It had been their third day 'in the field', as the lieutenant put it. Three days with his extravagant certainty trimmed back, three nights of sitting at the fire that burned high against the chill. There was though a subdued camaraderie among the men who sat about it on hauled logs or the heavy folded canvas they would later spread to sleep beneath. The shelters were well struck. The men had eaten well on fish, on potatoes and spinach taken onboard in Sydney, and Mr Jackson was generous with the porcelain jar he carried among them, chinking it against the rims of their tin mugs. There was talk of an axe that had disappeared from the camp during the day when it was deserted and the boy had been fishing, and one of the large pans brought across from the ship's galley. No one apart from the Scarborough lad, not even the lieutenant himself, appeared disturbed. The chance of petty theft, this distance from civilisation, was unlikely. The items would float back into view, Mr Jackson joked, as heads cleared in the morning.

Jean-Jacques sat a little apart from the crew, at the trembling edge of where the fire's leap extended. How different, he thought, men might seem when even slightly away from the authority that usually hemmed them in. The new sense of ease between them, the relaxed discipline of Mr Jackson, sitting with them in the circle of the fire, joining in their songs. These were not the shanties and chants Jean-Jacques was used to from occasional nights on deck, the raucous choruses, the thump of shouted refrains. There was a softness now in what they sang, homely verses that moved them from their daily guarded selves towards memories that, in the crammed living of seaboard life, were of the kind seldom spoken of. He supposed each must have a special place in mind, a village that defined them. Images that mostly he avoided returning to, freshly troubled him. The fear he had endured for those years that Mary had now told to others, in the book that was his life. The pursuit, the constant awareness of those who followed him, honed to do him harm. The face most of all he fought not to remember, the features close and peering at him with eyes no more benign than steel. The man in his white coat, returning his own dismay in those first minutes in which he knew he was not as other things about him, the first feeling of what it meant, to *be*; to know before the sounds were his to say so. *I am I*. When she had made him first himself. Her hands spread above the white pages where she would write him with such force that life might not be stopped.

He watched the shapes of the men move darkly against the rise of flames, the flow of light across their faces as they turned and laughed, or their expressions closed with the inwardness of thinking their own lives. Once he caught the glance of Mr Jackson directed towards him. For a few seconds, it may have been, the lieutenant who had been his friend, who had explained to him so much that pleased his mind, and touched his body in secret unexplained pleasure, seemed to look at him with the kind of warmth that once had been between them. Friendship. He had explained that word to him, as he had so many others. Words that now seemed shrivelled, as were smaller branches that fell from the fire and darkened as he watched.

One of the brothers turned and threw the remnants of a fish towards the animal that lay beside the sitting giant. A slight husky growl came from its throat, but it lay as it had been, its long legs laid side by side in front of it, its head intelligent and savage, its eyes reflecting the flames. It seemed to wait for some sign from the one being whose presence it acknowledged, whose will mastered its own. Only then did Dog leap forward as if a spring had been released. It devoured the fish in one circuitous leap that brought it back to how it had been, a swirl of haunches and wide gaping jaws, and then again it was almost as if a carved simulacrum of a sphinx. Mr Jackson continued to look at Jean-Jacques across the mastiff's granite repose. A thread of grief, was that too impossible a thing to imagine, from one to the other? A glance each may have preferred to hold, had the second mate not risen that instant and his figure cut between them, his reminding the men who looked to him that next day was make or break. Their last chance to track the great prize that, so he joked, had not drunk rum the night before as they had, so they dared not give it an inch. The lieutenant watched the night's prodigious glittering spill across the sky he had looked to early that morning as he raised the canvas flap. Once the prey was theirs. Once the other party returned with their new spar. He and Francis had talked of it, the humane and rational solution. The monster would survive, he guessed, wherever.

He would not be blood on their hands.

There was silence among the men next morning, beneath a uniformly dismal sky. The waters of the fjord slate grey as they climbed above it, the rise of the dark vegetation towards the jag of rocks and expanses of snow above. Mr Jackson had decided this last day they would take the other of the diverging tracks, as he liked to call those thinned ribbons between the shrubs that stood more than his own height, his reading into the compacted earth the likelihood that something other than weather and configuration had forced a way through. In his projecting of what there was such meagre reason to believe in, he imagined the huge barrel-bodied birds, their necks like magnified versions of that of an ostrich, their thighs compact and hard as boards, like those of the giraffe he once had run his palm against in the enclosure at Kew. The profligate variety of the natural world—only a fool might think there was an end to what yet might be subdued and caged and brought back to the docks of the scientific world. He had left a bosun's whistle with the boy who arranged and guarded the makeshift campsite on the pebbled beach. He had no wish to terrify the lad, but it had occurred to him that in such unexplored remoteness, where nothing might be thought impossible, such a creature as stalked his imagination may in some mischievous game have moved or filched, magpie-like, the shiny tinware the day before reported as mislaid.

The file of men climbed for well past an hour. There was little talk among them. They followed a different arrangement from the previous days; this time the machete wielder at the front, then the lieutenant with his loaded firing pieces, the man behind him with his waist ringed with hatchets. Each man carrying looped lengths of rope for the binding of the prey. The manacles the smithy clanked across his shoulders to confine the huge legs, once thrown from their balance. While several yards behind the rest, the giant who loped with Dog inches from his side, the great jaws muzzled with no more than a twined length of vine snapped from its climb against the trunk of a tree. It would not have held the mastiff's jaws for a second, should the creature be roused. But the sight of it assured the men it was under control. None but Mr Jackson understanding that it was the will of one ungovernable creature over another that so kept the panting hulk subdued. If it came to such a pass, it would be their combined wills that all would then depend on. He doubted that any of the men had thought it through as he had. But two contrary notions now coursed in his mind. An excitement, that persisted against all evidence, that he was on the verge of fame. While with it, not merely as a parallel possibility, but entwined as tightly as were the strands of the rope coiled across his shoulder, the sombre weave that, after all, was this the folly Captain Sharpe so clearly thought it was? One certainty filling his mind, the other depleting it.

There was a break in the vegetation that so far had crammed to either side of the file. In the sudden clearing to the left, the expanse of the fjord spread out beneath them, the pale line of open ocean between the jut of the distant Heads, the *Dorothea* motionless in its sheltered curve of land, the movement of small figures on its decks. 'Flies,' said one of the brothers, a word delivered with what Mr Jackson took to be a slur of contempt for how easily human strut might be diminished. He said, mildly, 'Ah, Harris,' in the tone of a disappointed parent. The men paused to wonder, to look out yet again at the immensity of where the captain's skill had brought them.

As they looked down to the craft that had brought them

this far, Captain Sharpe caught and held for the moment their pausing in the circle of his spyglass. Far figures, unaware of him, enlarged and held with that strange sense he had sometimes felt in one of his rare visits to a playhouse, of life reduced to some spectacle that is both believed in and yet so *performed*. Where is the line between what is truth, and what erases it? The reality of others? Without faith, what is anything—the fall of time, the saving of the minute, the tumble of all things, the churn of a Niagara as the end of all endeavour?

The captain detested the thoughts that came in on him. He was glad to lower his glass, to leave young Jackson and his believers on their distant pursuit. For a moment, in the sweep of his attending, he had glimpsed the great dog standing against the calf of its monstrous master, and had altered the slant of the brass tube so as not to see the distorted features of what came back to him. Now he walked across to the boy who was polishing one of the deck's lamps. He said kindly, wanting to feel the closeness of another human, 'The ship will shine like a jewel the way you're polishing us up there, Thomas.' One of the lads he had taken on from Grimsby, a pale reticent child when coming onboard, now as healthy a youth as his country could wish for. 'That's good of ye, sir.' The young face smiling but confused at being addressed by name, the old man watching him with his tired eyes. The boy lowered his head to cover his not knowing what else he might say. The captain stood for another moment, watching the boy's shy retreating into himself. He was oddly touched by it. He walked to the other end of the deck, considering how convention, how rank, set such barriers between men. Yet what else might be done, if the fabric of what we value was not to be fractured, savages as we would be among the ruins?

Francis Sharpe did not deceive himself about his own decline. He drew no distinction, as he thought of it, between how much was physical, the remnant of his fever, and the mental stress that came directly from what Christian charity had prompted him to take onboard. Sweet Jesus. He clamped his palm down on the extended tube, its brass segments sliding together. He walked to the starboard side of the deck. He looked with a longing that surprised him at the distant line of open sea. He glanced upward, accurately guessing the time now that the sun, through low cloud, appeared as a white disc. The smaller party that had set out that morning to draw water from one of the creeks, the other group selected some days ago to fell and work a replacement for the recently snapped spar, should return by late afternoon. He knew the men, once a suitable tree was found, would have worked quickly, preferring the ship's comforts to yet another night huddled against the shawls of rain that drew across the fjord, or the bitterness of when the skies had cleared, and the strewn hive of stars so easily turned from the delight they might fling out at other times, to the chilling force that entered each man's soul. The blade of distance, as the captain during his fever had thought of it, severing the cords of longitude and measurement, our days strapped to a whirling ball of trailing threads.

He returned to his cabin. As he entered, he touched the frame of the painting which a friend who had made the Grand Tour had given him when not much older than the boy there scrubbing at the lamps. He drew back from the thought of how the monster had so looked at it on those evenings, before the scales had dropped from his own eyes. How much of its true meaning might have penetrated that fearsome skull? He lowered the board of his desk from the

213

wall. He looked at the books that so mattered to him, the prized volumes of Cook, opened at entries for the days when the *Dorothea* now sailed the same waters. Above them, in a recess set into the panelling, other volumes he had shipped as indispensable. His Thomas à Kempis, in the tough serviceable binding his mother had hoped would weather his years at sea, the Douai version beside the more thumbed Vulgate, a history of the county where he had grown up, Shakespeare with slips of isinglass marking favoured pages, and a few other English classics, including 'Mr Pope, one of our own,' as his father had insisted on calling him. The three-volume novel Dorothea had kindly chosen for him.

The captain's vision blurred. Recently he had noticed how the eye he placed to the eyepiece, as he scanned the circle of reality the spyglass drew closer for him, wept after several minutes. It was something he had seen before, with older men, a junior in the service. A weakness of age, a warning signal of worse to come. The cabin was dark enough to need a lamp to read by. He was about to call for young Harry, then changed his mind. He took the decanter of burgundy from the clipped cupboard where he had placed it the night before. The wine black as he poured it. He sipped at it, then took what remained in the glass in one draught. He thought of the drive between the oaks up to the gravelled circle in front of Dorothea's favourite window, her contentment to look from it for hours at a time. Beyond a dip in the flowing line of the downs she so delighted in, the 'haul of the sea', as she once oddly put it. The phrase, from their first years together, had stayed with him. For most of their married life, her husband somewhere beyond its furthest line. His thinking of that now. He refilled his glass. The slow green slope from the coast, the balanced granite balls on the pillars before the drive between the oaks, the figure at the bow window watching for him. The neat script in the notebooks she carefully kept for him, so that later he might read of how life went on in its predictable seasonal turns, in this one spot.

Shreds of low cloud moved down from the peaks, covering and then revealing the sides of the fjord. Mr Jackson heard the panting of the men behind him as they ascended what may have been a track or the chance disposition of the foliage about them. Ahead of him, at times, the bite of the machete at an impeding branch. Few words were spoken throughout the last hour. Behind him, the soft clank of the manacles across the Scotchman's shoulders, the swish of shrubs bent back and then released. His mind played over the indisputable facts. The broken sack of ship's biscuits at the campsite. The slurred area where none of the men had walked, and yet so recently disturbed. His own certainty, for all the ill-humour that seemed to have descended on the men. He eased the weight of looped rope across his shoulder. His mind for the moment vaguely moving to a talk he remembered at a meeting of clever men in London. The press, the *smell*, of the occasion. There must have been light rain beforehand, for that odour was part of it too, the damp of uniforms and fine clothes, the tang of liquor as one passed certain groups, the soft lift of grey hair, even that he recalled, against the collar of the legendary Banks, bloated with fame and indulgent living, as he passed behind him. Mr Jackson mildly amused as the memory flicked across his mind, here of all places. As far from civilised discourse as a man might be. Yet the belief that he might spring such distances together! A slight smile as his hand ran the butt of the weapon he carried slantwise across his chest.

Then the sudden thump, the bounce of a dislodged boulder twenty yards ahead, the sound first of its impact on the steep slope above them, its swish against the low vegetation, its brief arcing appearance before its second impact, and then silence. The guttural rage of Dog as it strained against the chain it was held by. Because of his height, his advantage in seeing further than other men, Jean-Jacques saw in the swirl in the growth ahead of the file, the instantaneous appearance and concealment not of some hunted natural creature but a human form, the heavy swing of a woman's breast, the trailing of black hair, before the quivering of the bushes back to their stillness.

It was now as if time had entered its own distortion, seemingly slower as each fragment occurred but the quicker in its crammed sequence. The men called out and yelped as the mate, the only one apart from the huge figure behind them who had glimpsed a living being, shouted, 'It's it, it's it!' with an hysteria that ran its fuse along the group. Dog, crazed with excitement, the charged memory it carried of the hunts before its present life, the dark figures dissolving in the trees, the urging of settlers about him, the vast satisfaction of running quarry down. Its release from its leash however not leading it to ascend to where the fresh prey had been detected, but to the crewman with his axes as he climbed towards what he had seen. For Jean-Jacques' quiet command directed its massive bound. Its jaws clamped—as generations of breeding had prepared it—on the crewman's throat. The others of the party were now more terrified by that than attentive to the unseen but doubtless creature scrambling the incline above the track. The second mate, several paces off, saw how quickly death racked his contorted shipmate. The concussion of his discharged pistol rang back from the peaks, while Dog convulsed to the thinning echoes of the shot that had flung him back.

A pause then, remembered so differently by the men who would survive. A pause in which the afternoon's damp air was clawed at by the rasp of the wounded animal's breath, by the sobbing of one of the men whose nerves had collapsed at what could not be borne, and the thin high voice of Mr Jackson, who raised his firing piece to the slope above them, to where he believed he saw a rapid shivering of the bushes. Calling out in that broken voice, almost that of an adolescent, how what they had come so far for was *there*, as close at that, for Christ's sake! His shot smacked against a rock face; the bushes a few feet further along moved and stilled. He stood back to load again. One of the brothers fired both his pistols, seemingly at random. Mr Jackson stood close against the edge of the precipice. The barrel of his firing piece ran with the quicksilver of reflected sun. Jean-Jacques had made his way closer to the lieutenant. He saw sidelong the movement of another of the men close behind him. He heard the snap of the loaded gun. It was time enough. Time for him to signal Dog, with no more than a mild hissing of breath, for the animal to draw on the pits of resentment that so fuelled it, to raise itself on its one undamaged hind leg and hurl against the lieutenant its airborne weight, loading its paws against Mr Jackson's shoulders, to lurch and carry them both back beyond the track's edge, beyond the lip of the precipice. The same instant as another shot rang out, the ball from a pistol at close range drilled into the giant's shoulder, shattering the collarbone that once, far back, had been another man's.

Different men remembered differently. The surviving brother insisted he had attempted to follow the freshly murdering giant into the scrub and tangled growth he lumbered towards, after first stooping to take up the fallen pistol in the sweep of his hand. Another of the men recalled only his own rushing, and that of the men behind him, the slither of panic and noise and fear, as though dragged back towards the campsite on the beach by some tugging force.

The gunshots had cracked along the fjord. The captain stood and stretched his hands in front of him, barking his shin against the stove as he stumbled towards the door. The boy on deck turned to him with his face distorted, his words a garbled mix of vomit and confusion. For at the ring of the first shot the boy had looked up to the side of the tall hill where the captain, ten minutes before, had pointed to the hunting party through his spyglass before a shred of mist again concealed it. Young Thomas looked above the raw precipice of where the men must be, there or thereabouts. The puzzle of the merest second changing to the fact of what he saw, the distant falling blur and then the certainty of what it was, the plummeting not just of a man but of another creature too as if bound to him, their spiralling as they descended, their separating only as they were about to impact on the scrap of shore beneath them, the man head first, and springing apart from him, the dark spinning Dog.

The awful silence then in which the boy's sanity reeled. The captain's face so close against his own, shouting to him words that carried no meaning for him. The ship's cannon was fired for all parties to return at once. The surviving men from the failed hunt for the great and now forever unknown bird flung themselves into the ship's boat, and rowed the perfect calmness of the fjord, back to the high-riding craft that would bear them from what the captain, writing the one phrase in his journal that evening, would call, 'the dark centre of the sublime'. But first he would choose another four men, from those he valued most, to row to the edge where the boy had seen the figures fall, to gather the body from the rocks. He questioned the more coherent of the surviving crew, and rejoiced in their assurance that the monster, if he lived at all, would not do so for long. Another shot, one of the men lied to him, had shattered into his thigh. The dead crewmen on the mountain he could do nothing to retrieve.

For all its tragedy, the event worked as an elixir on him. His obligation to his men now drove him to his old efficiency, his pride in what it was to be an Englishman. When he addressed the men from the foredeck, they too felt the new force that came from him. He would be their leader as they had not quite known him, without Lieutenant Jackson so often serving as his delegate. He felt more substantial in his mind. In a week's time, he would have no qualms in once more opening the book that had so cast its shadow across their voyaging. Its evidence would mitigate whatever accounts might later be called for in London. He found he could look again at the Italian painting without the pangs it had earlier brought to him. But for the moment, his one thought was to sail from the fjord's confining vastness, to the once more consoling openness of the sea. It was early morning when the *Dorothea* unfurled its sails, and moved out from what James Cook had found a haven of rest.

The crew had expected the burial to take place on some spot on land, that deep instinct in each of them that this was how a man might choose to lie, given the final choice. A stone at least, painted with a name and date. But it was a deeper conviction of the captain's, the call to free his young relative forever from the marred Eden he had shared with his destroyer. So it was an hour's sailing south from the fjord's blunt entrance, and with the Lord's prayer recited by the men who had lived in community with him these past eight months, that Richard Jackson, aged twenty-nine, slid in his weighted canvas pod from the tilted board on the *Dorothea*'s leeward side, to what convention spoke of as repose.

III

Va. Said her name was Va, but not as other people tell their names. Her taking his hand and raising it and straightening one finger, and pressing it against her breast. She made the sound again, and then a third time, so he told it back to her, Va. Her then sliding his hand across her waist-length hair, along her side, across her nakedness. All that is her. So now he knows who she is. This is Va.

He lifted her own hand to run her fingers across the corrugations of his forehead. She reached high to touch his cheeks, to press against his throat. Her face was tilted that she might watch the movement of his lips. Ran her hands across his body, as he had done to hers. Jean-Jacques. He said it clearly, waiting for her to say it back. He moved her hand and told his name again. It might be too difficult, so he broke it in two, making it easier for her. Several times, his repeating it, as her eyes held his lips. Jean.

She touched his shoulder with her stretched hand, where three days before she had laid leaves on his gaping flesh, on the wound the first shot had burrowed into him. He could not imagine anything touching him so softly. He placed on hers his own hand, so much larger, yet so softly as he might. Then it is there, the sound she would use for him. Her lips pouted, the breath through her not quite touching teeth. *Je*, she mimicked him. Their first sounds that bound them. Va. Je. Va.

His shoulder, and the torn calf of one leg where another ball had entered, healed quickly. She was surprised that he stood and walked so soon. His face did not move as she had seen the faces of other men contort, when they felt pain. She had brought him back to the cave, above the track where the strangers had come and fought and killed each other, and where those who still lived descended back down to the beach and the boat they rowed to take them away. She had sat and watched him while he slept, and gave him water when he woke, but he desired nothing to eat, and slept again, until now, when they had looked at each other for a long time, before they told their names. She considered if he was a man like others, or a creature so much larger that was like them but not the same. It was later that the thought came to her as strangely marvellous, that she had not been afraid of him, even as he had crashed through the bush towards her then stood between her and the other men who had not followed as he had expected, but run away. Once he was sure they were not followed, he rested on the ground on his hands and knees. She had touched his shoulder, so he stood again, but stooped, and dragged his leg a little as she pointed ahead, and slipped through gaps in the bush that she knew, but where he must force a way for his hugeness.

On that first day, he lay in the part of the cave she had made soft with mosses and trampled pale grass. When he stirred and needed to drink she was not afraid to place her hand beneath his head, to help him. She held food to his mouth, a mixture of plants and fragments of meat. The first exchange of meaning then between them, when she thought he hesitated at what she offered him. He guessed it must be some kind of bird, because she had put her thumbs together, and moved her fingers like wings. He lay back and shut his eyes, not from any need to rest, but from the sense of peace that was new to him. He had liked it when her fingers flew for him. She watched until, when he woke on the third morning, he stood and looked from the mouth of the cave to where the *Dorothea* had anchored, but now there was only the long emptiness of the fjord beneath him. A fire was burning inside the mouth of the cave, and further in its recess, a larger area of blackened earth where another must have burned in the freezing months. The woman placed a piece of broken branch on the flames. He looked at the things he saw arranged in the cave. There were piles of mats that later he learned were made from the grey-green flax bushes, the stacks of dried and broken branches at the cave's furthest recess, but what held his attention were the few broken tools, a shattered axe, the tin mugs and basin he recognised as among the things taken from the camp below, when Mr Jackson had urged on his chosen crew with his talk of what they would hunt down and find such fame in.

There was also a folded square of canvas and a coiled loop of rope. In time he would learn how each had been come by—by chance, by scavenging, by theft. Only once, apart from the *Dorothea*, had she seen a ship enter the sweep of sea and land that she alone was part of. For several days men had axed down and shaped a long tree, and fashioned themselves a new mast. She had moved along the slopes above them, descending silently, close to where they worked. It was easy to help herself to the treasure they left about when they returned at dusk to their ship. The big knife she had close to her always. She had taken it along with a sailor's oil-stiffened hat, which later was lost when a blast of wind whirled it from her as she climbed to check on one of the traps she set for birds. She had drawn on the cave wall with a burned stick. Part of the drawing showed what looked like a hut made of grass, which was herself, her hair hiding her body completely. One day she saw him looking closely at it. He tapped the mound of grass and she pointed to herself and ran her splayed fingers through the fall of her hair, then her finger rested where his own still lay. It was the first time they laughed together, smiling the way men and women smile, and drawing close against each other. She then took a blackened stick from last night's fire and did another picture for him. This time it was some kind of four-legged creature, its ears two tiny triangles, its mouth carrying a broken line that became an open mouth. She moved her hands and moved two fingers to show running away. A cat the men had brought ashore with them and that she tried to bring back home. But the cat ran away from her. They laughed again and she leaned in against the man.

As yet there was not the means to ask about deeper things. He wondered at everything about her. As she too of him, this new kind of man she had brought to where she had lived and survived, although apart from the seasons turning in their cycles, which she felt as part of her blood, the passing of time was inseparable from its long receding hollowness back to the yellow beach, back to the ships that carried her, back to the pouring fire, and the long walking towards where there was nothing further to move on to. So far from everything that the days or weeks were of little account to her, when to survive the present was her one demand.

There were times when she thought he slept, but the new kind of man lay awake. He closed his eyes when he felt she was observing him. But as she herself slept, or moved about the cave, there was a pleasure in watching her. In the dark of night, when she added to the almost spent fire, the light leaped and shivered across the irregular walls, and he would delight in a thing so simple as that. Everything that surrounded her, the harsh simple comforts of where she had lived for so long she could not assess, brought on a sensation that at times bewildered him. It was a feeling those evenings of knowledge in the captain's cabin had never touched on. A way of looking at her so carefully it was as if he was drawing something from her into himself. He wondered at how she might be as she was, one side so vastly different from the other. Seemingly one woman from this side, another from that, as she moved and turned. He recalled one evening, a few days out from the colony called New South Wales. The two men were speaking of untrue things that sailors often swore were true, shapes that were women but also fish, of voices that called across calm seas that led ships towards whirlpools. One might make a book of them, the captain had said. And they had talked then of how the word 'mystery' might mean something to one man that another believed too obvious to question. 'A word worth remembering,' the captain had joked to him, 'when Mr Jackson's rationality breaks down.' But then a disagreement between the two which Jean-Jacques failed to understand, the older man insisting revelation was of another order entirely. Words that had whirled about him and he had thought long forgotten, yet such confusions troubled him now when he slept badly, and sank into the untrue imaginings of dreams, where words lost certainty as surely as a fleeing man might slip on ice. The woman who tended him caught up too in such distortions, until so soon, it seemed yet another wonder, the ease each began to find in an understanding that was not fenced in with speech.

Va at his side both day and night. Va and Je later, together, as she showed him the vastness of where she lived, the tracks and places she alone might visit. When signs and expressions, and rapid sketches on sand or the cave walls, allowed their minds to meet. For her to tell her story. At times anger came down on him, the kind of rage that had driven him so long ago, the urge to destroy what so seemed to exist for no other purpose but to thwart him. All things fashioned to hate, to be hated in return. She delayed her story at such times, to soothe him. To draw him back to now. Now which is only because of then. Their foreheads leant towards each other to touch. The woman whose face from one side was smooth as the skin on the inside of her arm, as was her breast, the shoulder he put his lips to, the thigh one opened hand moves across. But not yet Va, until her head drew back to smile up at him, his looking now at the tightened pull of her other cheek's discoloured muscle, the stained grooves running the length of her throat as though a claw had scored it. On that side too the fall of her breast, the flesh running beneath it, as if partly formed from twisted leather, her buttock torqued and wrung with scarring. His hugely knuckled hands held her towards him. It was her completeness that delighted him. I am this and that, her appearance said to him. He did not yet have a way to tell her, she had given him back to himself.

Over the months they found there were ways to know each other, other signs they invented. He thought of what he once saw so far back. The pictures in his mind were tiny, distant, arriving from so far. A man and a woman happy together, the strangeness of it as it had come to him. The word he remembered for it. The notion to be free in choosing always with another. Marriage for choosing, married for what they were. As he and Va now were. He showed her to place her hands on his wrists, to stretch her fingers so they reached a fraction of the way encircling them. As his own hands enclosed hers, her forearms so slight inside his folding fists. She comprehended what this meant. Each belonging to the other. She watched his lips and breathed the sound she thought must follow his. *Ma*, she said. *Je* and *Va* and *Ma*.

There was no haste in what they did, in their walking hills or beaches, her showing him where things were found that they might eat, the ways to catch fish, the racks she built from interlacing branches, where fish were dried, or the spread pelt of the rare seal she was quick enough to kill. The way she set the delicate traps for the smaller birds, the tangled snares for seabirds. He admired whatever she did. He learned to choose the right flax and cut it with the machete one of the sailors had dropped, when fear had dragged them back to the boats. They laughed when she held against him the clothes she had made from the softened weave of the flax, and the jacket cut from the seal. He collected in the summer months the wood they soon enough would need for their fires. For weeks he laboured to hollow out a fallen trunk, and placed projecting frames from smaller branches to either side for balance.

Almost a year had passed before the now many signs they had made together, and the pictures she had drawn for him, allowed her story to be told so he understood.

There is a girl on a beach so shining that when much later a man will cross the world to paint one of the hundreds like it, it will seem more than gold, but shadows will have entered into it, along with the colours of life, and the loveliness of what those who wish it there, will see. That is the beach where the girl begins.

She is a girl who watches carefully, and quickly learns from what older women do, but is less at ease with those her own age. She does not hear the surf as she walks on the beach, nor what sound it is when the palms move in the wind and seem to walk against the sky. When she lies down to sleep at night, she thinks of what she has seen, the movement of the air against her skin and catching her hair, and the dipping of branches against her. She does not know what sounds are like. People are kind to her when she is a child, and some less kind when she is finer-looking than her sisters. She cannot dance and sing as other girls do. She has a way to tell what she is thinking by the way she moves her hands, but not everyone has time to understand. She knows when people laugh at her, and when they do things with her because her silence makes them bold. She is allowed to look after animals, and that makes her happy, and she is the one who kneels for a long time to clean fish when they are brought ashore. When her mother dies she is more alone. She sleeps in the corner of the house where her mother lay, and thinks how they would say things with their hands no one else knew.

Then so much happens, so quickly. The men are fighting with strange men from another place, the women hide in the trees on the side of a steep hill, but she is caught because she has not heard them coming at her. She is sent from one man to another. Then she is on a big ship and her own people are further away each day. The warm days fade and there is a long time when it is cold, and then the sun comes again. When she has a child and it is too small to stay alive she sees it dropped from the side of the ship when the sea is calm and she sees it sink slowly until she can no longer see it. She thinks she will jump into the sea, and will be left alone, but is too afraid. She is sick then and the ship no longer has room for her. When it meets another ship she is put in a small boat and rowed across to it, and is a present for them. The new ship is smaller but the men who live on it often fight among themselves, and drink what makes them angry, and push at her to make her dance. One night when it is dark and a fire leaps about their own dancing she falls against a big boiling pot as the boat moves from under her, and it tilts over as she grabs at it and she knows the skin is being peeled from her. She thinks the fire is eating her. She remembers only dark for a long time, and then comes back to herself. (She tells this to Je by drawing the lines that mean herself, and rubbing them out, and raising all her fingers, then drawing the lines again.)

One of the men is kind to her. Some of them want to throw her from the ship. They hate to look at her. But because they are now close enough to land to see the broken black line of hills, they decide to take her there, and leave her on a beach that is rock and ugly sand. The one kind man, who looks so different from the others (with eyes like this—she draws the corners of her own so they are tilting upwards), gives her a jacket and a knife and some ship's biscuit, and a container for water. She is rowed towards the beach and left in the tumble of surf and thinks she will die. The marking down one side still sharply pains at different times. It does not sadden her that she will die. She finds a place to shelter near the rocks above the sand, and there are big clumps of yellow grass like hair, she thinks, rising up from people's heads beneath the ground. She tries to eat some bread from her jacket pocket that the sea has ruined. She lies on the mounds of grass and when she wakes the sky is clear and she is cold, yet the marvellous feeling that she is alone, as she has not been now for so long. *I am my own.* She will begin walking, and stay alive. She will suck at the seabird eggs she finds and although the flesh tastes bad, the carcass of a seal pup prevents her starving. There are shells she opens with the knife or crushes with a stone. She kills a bird with a fractured wing. She chews on bark when there is nothing else. There is a place where she sees smoke in the distance, and hides, and guesses there are people moving ahead on a track. When she comes to the dead fire where the smoke came from, she finds scraps of cooked meat. No, she cannot guess how long, how far, how high she may have had to climb in summer months. She is expert now at surviving, at knowing what plants to eat, how by sitting still for half a day she might snare one of the fat pigeons. Once she finds a dead man who may have fallen from a cliff, and she takes the useful things that are still with his body. His stone adze, the shaped hooks in a pouch about his neck, a cloak folded and tied about his waist.

Her body becomes stronger. She can walk or climb many hours at a stretch. She was still young when she came to where there was no further land to cross, where she had made her home. She looks at her body and guesses she is the age perhaps of her mother, when she died.

When she comes to the end of what there is to tell, she makes a joke. She draws a sketch of steep slopes and a peak, and sits astride him as she likes to do, and points to the drawing and to him, and back again. This is the end of the story. He is her mountain.

Va waited across the months, and then the years, for Je to tell him more of himself, until it seemed not important to her. What she knew of him, what each day confirmed, was enough. She did not attempt to think beyond that. What scrap from before they were together could be of importance, now there was nothing more she might want? There were few signs, no drawings, for all that might be meant by *before*. They were together each minute of night and day. Through the turning of the seasons, the pull of the stars to different patterns, there is only *this, as we are.* Her sitting astride him, her hands spread and pressing on his chest, so at times he thought what could not be told, thought of the white hands spread across the book in front of Mary in the picture, the pages beneath her hands; the story that even at the end of the book Mr Jackson told him of, was not the end of the story. His surviving the ice, and all that is new begins, as it began again when the *Dorothea* moved on to the other ice, at the other end of the world, and left him, as the captain must have wanted it, to die. But he was her story and she wrote it still. She made him breathe and so must want him to keep on. But when he lay at night and Va slept against him, when he heard her own breathing bring such calm to him, when *this is what Ma means*, he thought, and their closeness was as if one had become the other, his mind grew heavy with the mystery of it.

Time which matters to us, he wanted to make clear to her. Even when we think it does not. We are part of it when we are most free. He had drawn a circle in the dust, and his finger made a small mark on its rim, almost at the bottom of its roundness. But Va looked at him and moved her head as she did when she had not understood. This was in the early part of their being together. He had then found an overhang of rock that kept a shelf beneath it dry, and gathered stones of different sizes to arrange on it. He set them out to instruct her, and to remind himself. He showed her a little of what the captain had explained to him, moving stones about a larger stone as he pointed to the sun, and to a small white stone that was the moon. This other stone which was almost round, and was there, where he stamped his foot, and opened out his arms to take in what surrounded them, what they looked down on. The movements that never stopped. All this is theirs, and they belong to it. He was unsure how much she shared with him, but she smiled as he showed her. Yes, some of it, surely. The picture coming to him of the way a stone so rings out beyond itself, dropped in quiet water. There were stones set in rows on the ledge, then smaller rows to speak for the months, for the years since he arrived. This part of his telling she was quick to follow. Two stones from now, the heavy snow would cover the black peaks, and might come so far as where they stand. Six stones, and they would not feel hungry, and kill a new seal, and paddle on the hollowed log to different coves, and birds would be easy at that time to snare, after the weeks when they gathered eggs from near the shore, and on the steep slopes. The times for the roots and the small plants she knew to find. After their months spent mostly in the cave, with the fire always burning, the days when they made mats together and clothes from the softened flax and were content to lie for days with the speechless companionable certainty of fellow animals, the world was freshly theirs. And so it goes.

So it goes until one of the tremors that sometimes moved beneath the cave became the great rocking of the fjord and its mountains. For several days the sudden jerking of the earth returned, the rush of loosened rocks and broad sliding fans of hillside, that left the air heavy with dust. As they left the cave they found small slips across tracks they knew, and their pool for collecting fresh water sealed beneath a boulder. And their library of stones was lost. The brow that had protected it had broken loose, and debris poured down to smother it. Va watched Je's face, fearing how the loss would sadden him. She understood how the rows of stones held fast the patterns that must be remembered, as she herself did the ways to cut and soften and plait the strips of flax to what it was she needed.

He stood beside her looking at the sloping piled mass of rock, then turned so he faced the length of the fjord, its waters now spread with the blueness of the sky and the sun's broad reflecting streak. He raised his arms and his mouth opened and she felt with her hand against his side the vibrating of his roaring out to everything their eyes took in. She feared it was a cry of pain she was unable to understand, the gathering of everything in that huge indomitable body that raged and defied. And so it had been as it first racked through his throat and dragged the air from his lungs. She watched and pitied and feared for him. Her thought entirely being how so willingly she would take it on herself, the pain she feared for him. She would take it and suffer it for him, had that been possible. But then a strangeness even beyond that. The sudden falling of his arms, his great hands opened and relaxed. He turned to Va, raising his hands to her shoulders, looking down to her face, and laughed with a kind of furious delight. For it had struck him that how others define time, that too had been taken from him. Was there any freedom left he did not possess? An elation that brought with it the physical sensation that he was not at that moment standing above the fjord, but was raised over it. The dreadful error, as time in time brings home.

One year became five, those five then ten. The worst of facts came in on him—that what was true for him may not be so for Va. Everything shared but that. He had seen the marvellous blackness of her hair, its shine in even diminished light, change to like the sky can sometimes seem, the run of greyness before the dawn has truly come. One day to carry the big flax bag she took for foraging, for finding fallen wood

233

she brought back, whatever season of the year, so suddenly too much for her. Yet not so rapidly as that. The increments of age, so unobserved, and then their shackling. The winter when her shoulder ached so badly as the snow first came to the peaks, while the rain kept on for weeks. The long months as the soreness in her side became more, a pain which at times prevented her standing alone. It was soothing to lie on the wide bed they had made from mats and layered grasses, the fire burning day and night for her, as the walls of the cave glinted with runnels of seeping water hardened into ice for these, the coldest months.

They seldom needed the signs that had so become part of them. It was as if the body of each of them felt so instinctively for the other's as well. They were seldom further apart than an arm might reach. It was Jean-Jacques who now wove the flax in the daylight hours, and at times in the night, with the fire's redness wavering over his tilted face, intent on what he did. The shadow he cast was huge on the uneven, sloping walls. Should he look up from the movement of his fingers, the woman was watching him, her eyes quickened with the fire's reflection. She had not asked what he was doing, because there would be purpose to it, and when he meant her to know he would show her.

The thought came to him on a day when the rain stopped, and the sun shone through for several hours, and it was less cold outside the cave than it had been for many weeks. They would walk at least a little way. He had fed her dried fish and boiled eggs with his own fingers, as so long ago she had done for him. They smiled as each remembered. It was not necessary, but each took pleasure in it, so it became a game between them. Yes, it was a good day for them to walk the tracks. Perhaps to descend to the stony beach where she would wait and watch him sit across the floating log, and take it out a little into the fjord, and bring back fish. But after they were halfway down, she leaned against him, and he felt her frailty. He carried her back to the cave, and returned to take the new fish he had promised her. It was while his legs thrust back the water, and the log moved out into the cove, that the thought came to him. The canvas hammocks shaped like half a moon that the sailors had slept in on the ship. They were in his mind as he walked back with the fish he cooked in embers he drew aside from the fire. But this was not, as he had hoped, the beginning of the changing season. The rain fell again so thickly that everything beyond the cave blurred behind it. Snow came back. Va lay and watched him as he cut the flax she had woven into shapes she did not understand, but was content to watch. He drew the twine woven from strands of different vines through holes he made in the flax, and tied with knots she had not known. When they chanced to meet each other's gaze, his fingers lifted slightly from his work, before he again lowered his head. Then one day the weather changed again and the winter was over, and the air felt as if it arrived from warmer places. They stood in the space in front of the cave. They closed their eyes and the sun moved over them.

He showed her what he had made. It was a woven cradle that could be slung across his shoulders, the narrow ends tied so that it hung in a deep loop where he would carry her. Any place they had walked together for so long, they would visit still. She made the sign to indicate she would be like a child, and he nodded back at her, and they would fish, and check the snares, and gather eggs and plants, and even carry wood as they had always done. And to continue the work she had begun perhaps a year before, after they had seen a ship enter the fjord. Va had been the one to see it first. An autumn morning with a drizzling rain, that made things seem as though looked at through a veil. Another of those sparse images came back to him from so long before he had become Jean-Jacques, of women he had seen in a procession, behind a long box drawn by horses, while there were men and soldiers looking for him, and he had waited, concealed in a high broad tree, until the procession had passed by, and the dark came down. The women's faces behind veils, and the sound too came back to him, a bell so different to the one that is rung on ships, a slow booming that hung in the air, and slowed the people walking. But it was a distant bell, of the kind he was used to, that made him look down through the fine web of rain to see a ghost ship, as the sailors on the *Dorothea* would have called it, riding on the sea that was the same colour as the mist.

He and Va watched for the three days as it waited for its crew to row back their barrels of water, and the chock of axes had come up to them. By the time it sailed, the weather had cleared. It was not a ship of whalers, or explorers. It rode higher in the water; there were portals along its sides where the muzzles of guns might quickly be exposed. Through the glass he kept raising to examine it, he saw there were men wearing uniform. Yet a strangeness about the craft, as if there were too few crew for what it was. He thought perhaps some kind of plague had ravaged it, or it was badly off course. There would have been no comfort for it, had it hoped to find fruit or animals in their scouring of the coves. The flag at its stern was not one he knew.

Once the ship had left, Va wondered at how solemn he seemed for several days. She was alert to his moods, to the few times when something seemed to disquiet him. At night he lay stroking her hair until she slept. Then with the stick drawings on the scuffed earth that they had come to need less and less, he made it clear that yes, the sudden appearance of the visitors was on his mind. He began at once to go about what he explained to her. The iron stakes for the cage that so far back the lieutenant had brought ashore, the great mallet and shorter metal lengths—all left in panic as the surviving men withdrew—he had within weeks wrapped in canvas from the makeshift shelters. These he had laid in clefts above the water line. He lugged and angled rocks to protect the items as well as he might from the elements and the gnaw of the salt air. There had been no call for them until now. Many had rusted, some had rotted wafer thin, and crumbled as he raised them. But enough, he thought. There is enough here to help with what he had in mind.

Va reminded him how no more than a few ships had entered the fjord since his own arrival. No one knew they were here. They understood where they lived as no one else might comprehend. They grew old but nothing worse might happen to them. They were Je and Va. Was that not enough? It is always enough, he told her. But he would risk nothing that might disturb her. And so for the summer months, and into the time when the black heights began to be hooded in white, he would carry her in the cradle he had made for her, and she would rest her head against his chest as they walked the network of scarcely perceptible paths, and hear the beating of his heart, and give him the things to eat she had carried for him, and the container for water that had been hers since she was put ashore, oh so far back, burned and left to die, but Je too was making his way towards her, and so they were here together, as he carried rocks and piled them at places he decided on.

Defences, he called them, and explained so she understood. He chose places where the slopes were steep. He set them above false tracks rising from the shoreline, hacked out with the machete that had been within inches of descending on him when he had crushed the skull of the always quiet German who had swung it at him. There were a dozen places where he piled heavy rocks and proved them together with smaller chunks until their stack was as tall as himself. He calculated their balance, the pressure needed to release them. Va sat on the slope above him and watched his naked back gleam with sweat. The mottled piecing of his flesh altered as he turned, as shadows flexed across him. When he paused to take the water she held towards him, he blocked the sun from her with his bulk. As he moved so that once again the light fell on her, she raised her hands, palm upwards, their sign from the beginning, to tell how good things were. *I am happy.* His hand touching her head, before he took up one of the iron bars. He angled one end so it lodged between the cairn of rocks. The rest stood out so it might when necessary be levered. The rocks would totter and lose their piled firmness and vault down on the path twenty yards beneath, fanning out, gathering force, as they fell.

Over the summer he laboured at a dozen similar constructions. Always he carried Va in the cradle that he set close to where he worked. When he had used the few iron struts that had not corroded, he chose branches that he broke and trimmed and shaped so they served the same intent. Some of the cairns he set where he believed they might carry more of a mountainside down with them, as they poured on whoever attempted to come near. It would seem as though nature intended the shuddering leap of their descent.

As the summer days reached their length, then the warm

weeks when slowly they drew in, before the suddenness of another season with its first blast of cold and an early sheeting of the higher slopes with snow, a different quietness came to the giant figure and the woman he carried always with him, across the raw terrain they had made their own. Je and Va. She became less well. She coughed at night and when she stood and attempted to walk, he would circle her with his arm, guiding her. He was glad when she now slept longer, and when the pain in her side troubled her he drew her close against him, stroking her hair, the skin of her shoulder ruckled beneath the gentleness of his fingers. His lips against her face, so she knew from how they moved that he was saying over and again her name. Tenting her hand inside his own, he would say the other word she knew by the shaping of his mouth. He would tell her 'Ma', which meant everything they were, or might ever be, one to the other.

His own thoughts, as he lay and the fire glimmered down, that he neither feared nor drew comfort from, but knew with a new dark clarity what must come. He recalled the far back morning when the recess, where he had made time into a picture of stones for her, was no longer there. His shame at how, for those few agitated minutes, what could never be had seemed as if it could, and a madness in him said, we are free of it now, there is no more time. Yet behind all else, there moved now the appalling certainty of what had not before come to him. The fact that he remained unchanged, while others aged. That he would live as certainly as others died. How might he remain as always he had been, while Va grew frail, as even trees at last lost strength, as iron flaked towards what it was not? All things to end, Je thought, because they start as things must start. *But I did not.* A word that need never be, but then a mark is made on an empty page. *And I have begun.*

In the dark, he runs his hands across his head, lets them lie along his face, the tilting of his jaw. He stands, anxious not to wake Va, who lies curled into herself, as sleeping animals lie, in self-content. The first lightening of the sky above the mountains, as he has seen it so many times. He stands looking down on the darkness as it slowly releases the fjord. Soon the long inlet of sea will rise with its own light, the coves take definition, the peaks stand black. His own life, as it comes to him now, is all one person has to see again. He has the feeling, which Mr Jackson would have smiled at and called mere superstition, that the black ship with the covered guns will come again. If not that, another. When the next summer comes he will return to his defences. He will carry Va, as he had done this year. He will make the sentence last forever. And something of what he was before the ice, he knows is there still, for he is all things that already he has been. He has walked to the first cairn, and back. He stands at the lip of the cliff and speaks aloud. 'Mother,' he says, 'write this: there will be blood.'

Va is watching for his return. He stirs the embers of the fire between the small mounds he has made so the pan for water can be placed across them. He cooks the pigeons' eggs he will then peel and hand to her. While the water heats she beckons him to kneel beside her. She had wondered where he was. She places her fingers tightly around his wrist as far as they will go. The sign they have used together for so long. 'Don't go,' it says.

'Never,' he tells her back, circling her wrist.